DEATH

on the

DOWNBEAT

DEATH on the DOWNBEAT
BLUEROOMBOOKS.COM
DECATUR, GEORGIA
978-1-950729-13-5

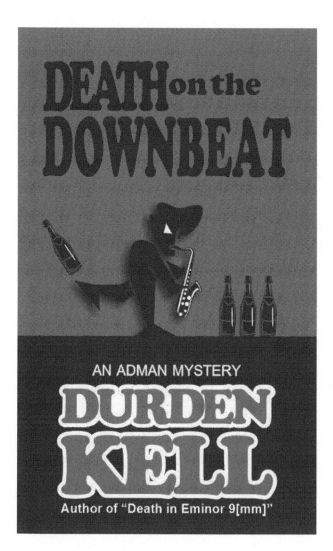

Prelude

"Next!"

Everyone in line stepped forward. One toward the counter. That left two people ahead of her. Two more before she reached the window at the post office and could mail the first package.

"Next!"

One more ahead of her now. One more before she could let her gift begin winging its way to deliver the beautiful surprise.

"Next!" said the man behind the counter, waving for her to step his way.

She felt a rush of excitement and stepped forward. She set the USPS official box on the counter. "Here you go. These are books. Please send them Media Mail." She smiled sweetly, eyes twinkling in pure innocence.

The man behind the counter saw her smile and, like all men did with her, couldn't help himself and smiled in return. She was sweet, innocent, and sexy, all at the same time. He put the package on the scale and punched a few buttons.

"Look at the screen, please, and answer the question. Thank you," he fairly crooned.

She turned to the screen which read: Was there anything breakable, poisonous, explosive, fragile, liquid…blah, blah, blah? She punched No, then looked up and smiled again.

"And you say this is books? Media?"

She nodded in the affirmative.

"Need it delivered by a certain date? Insured?"

She dipped her chin so her eyes were looking up at him, shook her head in the negative. He almost melted where he stood. Punch-punch.

"Thank you. Can you confirm this address is accurate?" He turned the box around for her to look. She pulled out a piece of paper, conferred, then nodded. He smiled. "Umm…do you…uh…do you need this delivered by a certain date? Haha! I already a-a-a-asked that. Haha!"

She gave a little shrug, batted her eyes. "No, thank you. When it gets there is when it gets there."

Oh, Lord. He was so very happy to be standing behind the counter. He punched another button and a label printed showing postage paid and delivery ZIP. He slowly stamped MEDIA MAIL all over the box. Each thrust of the stamp's plunger not helping his libido stay in control as he imagined…

Whoa. Back to business, he said to himself.

"That will be seven dollars and eighty-five cents. Cash, debit, or credit?"

"Cash, please." She handed him a ten — fingers lightly but innocently clumsy of course — brushing his hand. His hands shook as he counted out the change into her sweet little palm. He twisted on his stool and reached behind, ripped the receipt from its printer and grabbed a highlighter. He whipped around in a manly fashion and set the receipt on the counter, turning it toward her. Her eyes followed the highlighter he used to then circle a number.

"We would appreciate it if you could take this survey and tell us how your service was today."

Her eyes raised again. She slowly slid the paper from under his fingers. "Of course. Anything to help out my most favorite Guy in Powder Blue. Oh, and by the way, could you also mail this."

He took the envelope. "Of course I can mail it for you. Hahahaha. Th-th-that's, you know, what we do here." He glanced at it. "Ah, you are donating to the local animal shelter."

"That's right. It's a no-kill shelter. I do not believe in killing animals."

He watched as she turned and sashayed away. Obediently, customers in line did not move until commanded. A few seconds went by, then they heard "Next!"

Killer Jams

On Wednesday nights, two Jazz Jams run concurrently. I'd usually hit Après Diem first, arriving by eight-thirty, and sit in with the house band. Misha was on keys there each week. Yeah. A paying gig. Then around ten-thirty I'd drive one mile down Monroe to Amsterdam and sit in at Red Light Café, or RLC as regulars called it.

J Nick had run the RLC jam for five years but when he was murdered, the owner, Michael, asked if I'd run it. I had too much going on to properly do it every week, but subbed occasionally. I mostly show up at jams for chinwags with folks I don't get to see very often, to play, and to scope out new talent from Young Lions lining the walls.

So on this Wednesday night, I again put Sweet Stella, my sax, in the backseat and left The Farm at seven-thirty heading for Midtown. This time of day traffic is at the tail end of a rush hour, so going into the city and, having been born and raised here, I knew how best to get around the bottlenecks at any time of day.

When somebody new to Atlanta asks how long it takes to get from Point A to Point B, we natives' first question is, "What time of day will you be going?" Newcomers do not understand and often get their backs up like we're messing in their business. They'll say with more than a bit of attitude, "What does it matter what time of day I'll be going?" Then we natives will say, "Oh, you're new here. Let me 'splain how it is."

They never believe us. Ever. Give them a month and they change their tune.

I arrived at Après Diem exactly at eighty-thirty. As usual, Misha was hollering over the top of the bar to one of the Heathers that worked there. "Iss verry goot, yes? Okay. I have that. Quick, quick! I got to play!"

I pushed him toward his keys. "I'll bring it to you. You're wanted on stage and your adoring fans are calling."

Misha laughed at the adoring fans comment, but did as he was told. A few minutes later one of the Heathers handed the cold brew across the bar and I schlepped it over to the stage and put it down next to the wall so Misha wouldn't kick it with his feet. I make such a good mother, don't I? Actually, I'm just protecting the electronics. Only newbies — or the very drunk and/or passive aggressive — set their drinks on top of equipment.

"Adman! Wanna play?" Dave asked. Dave runs this jam.

"Yessir!" I answered and walked back to one of the Heathers and ordered coffee and biscotti. I would get my usual at RLC later.

"Hey, Adman," one of the Heathers said. "Where you gonna be sitting?"

I pointed to an empty stool at the bar near the drink station.

She nodded and said, "Not having your usual tonight?"

Shook my head no. Fifteen minutes later freshly brewed coffee and biscotti arrived, but I was playing and it would have to wait. When I finished there were shouts of *Adman! Adman!* I took a bow, putting all the comedy I could into it so folks would laugh. By ten-thirty I had played one more time, paid my check, then slid on out, headed to RLC.

Mitchie was at the door, as usual. And per our usual if I showed up late, he let me slide on in, waiving the cover. Standing just inside the door, I turned toward the stage. The bandleader was blowing his trumpet. I watched him; waved when he turned my way. His name was Mark Hamill (what were his parents thinking?), so naturally everyone called him Skywalker. Michael, the owner with his wife Ellen, saw me coming and arched a brow and pointed a finger that was our code for *Your usual?* I nodded. Young Lions held out fists for me to bump when I went by and I did to echoes of "Hello, Adman" and "Hey, Adman". Finally made it to the bar in the back where a Jack Daniel's Black American over ice was awaiting me.

"Hey, Michael. Thanks," I said and we touched glasses in cheers. We both sipped; me the Jack, Michael a fresh expresso.

"Start a tab tonight?"

I nodded in the affirmative. My phone vibrated with an incoming text. It was CC.

Hey there, you *[her favorite nickname for me that I will not mention to you as I am a gentleman]*. Love you. Wake me up when you get home. Mama be needing her loving man.

Hello daddy, this was gonna be a good evening fer-shure-fer-shure. I put the phone in my pocket.

"Hey, Adman. You gonna play tonight?"

Standing before me was Roxanne Robards, Ro-Ro by nickname. When it comes to double bass players in the Jazz world, females exist, but there aren't a lot of them. She was one. To look at her you wouldn't think she could handle such a big instrument, but the girl knew her stuff. I call her girl because she's petite and doesn't look older than fifteen at first glance. She is thirty-one. I know this because she told me what year she was born and I'm good at easy math and counting on my fingers, so figured it out pretty quick.

I did not hug her because there's one other thing I knew about Roxanne. She was a man-eater. Sure, she looked innocent enough, but hiding in her eyes was a streak of cruelty that could deliver pain. Now, if a guy and a gal like pain, then that's their business. I was not one who liked pain and was not going to even pretend she turned me on.

Which she didn't.

"I was thinking about it. How about you?"

She turned toward the stage and giggled, "I've already played once. Maybe Skywalker will invite me up again. Hey," she said, laying a strong hand on my arm, "maybe you can play with me, too. Remember that thing we did a few months ago?"

I smiled. That was awesome. See, on the stage she could give the bass as much pain as she wanted. She could treat it mean. Why, the audience loved it, the meaner the better. What happened was that we were playing this song…what was it? Oh, yeah. It was called "Don't Let This Smile Fool Ya", a song by my friend and songwriter Ruby Grace.

"Hell, yeah. Too bad Ruby isn't here to sing it like she was that night." I shook my head.

Roxanne did the same. Then she snapped her fingers like she had a bright idea. "We could just play it. We don't need the words. I've got the chart. I'm sure you do, too, right, Adman? On your iReal Pro on your phone?"

"Sure. We could do that. Hey, here comes Skywalker. Let's ask him what he thinks." I called him over and explained the situation.

"Hell yeah. That would be great. How about Little Man on drums? And uh…let me think… keys …how about Ty?"

Roxanne and I looked at each other and back to Skywalker. Between us we gave two thumbs-up; he went to set it up while the singer on stage finished with "Bésame Mucho", a song written in 1940 by Mexican songwriter Consuelo Velázquez. In 1956, Sunny Skylar wrote the English lyrics. Skywalker thanked the singer as the crowd applauded. She bowed to the audience, blew kisses at each player, and stepped down out of the spotlight.

"Let's get Little Man up here. Little Man? Where are ya? Come on up." Skywalker held a hand above his eyes to shade the light. "And let's get Adman and Ro-Ro up, too. Ty, you want to stay up?"

Ty nodded. Skywalker said, "Adman, how you want to do this?"

I hollered out, "Down and dirty. That all right with y'all?"

The audience hollered approval and Ty grinned. Skywalker said, "Alrighty then. Let's do 'Don't Let This Smile Fool Ya'. It was written by our very own Ruby Grace who is not here to sing it tonight, but we'll get by."

Twenty crazy minutes later we hit the final notes hard. Ty was in a delirious sweat after bringing in some New Orleans sensibilities. Little Man's eyes were rotating wild. Ro-Ro was cussing with joy. And I was on a natural high with the audience. Too bad Michael couldn't bottle that because he would surely be pocketing some coin. What a fun night.

I paid my check and left RLC around midnight. They were still going strong, but I was hoping I didn't wear myself out too much so that when I got home I still had the energy to wake up CC, iffen ya knows whut I mean.

"Hello, my name is Adman. I play the saxophone."

You might be wondering who I am. In case you missed it in the newspaper stories about the murder trial a few years ago, my wife, CC, and I were star witnesses. My name is John Cold Dann, but friends and fans call me Adman. I play the saxophone. Some tease me and say I also play The Star and I say, "Dang straight. Somebody's gotta do it, so why not me?"

My wife's name is Clarissa Celeste Caruthers; she kept her professional name at work. She's a paralegal in a huge law firm that takes up three floors at the top of a high-rise at Atlantic Station. We've been married now a little more than two years after dating for three and being engaged for two. Friends call her CC, like I do, but I call her Mrs. Adman, Honey Bunny, Love Muffin, and other such as is deemed appropriate for the moment. Only in private, mind you.

No, I will not tell you what she calls me in private. A man's got his dignity.

I was born and raised in the Great State of Georgia, in the far southwest outreaches of Metro Atlanta in a small town called Sharpsburg. Mom and Dad and my siblings still live there. Let me take a moment to bring you up to current times.

CC and I were held hostage in my house by a serial killer who murdered three Jazz Cats and one Jazz Kitten, but we overpowered him. By "we overpowered him" I will give credit where credit is due. Twas CC who threw the pot of hot coffee in his face before I tackled him, took away his 9mm, and held him while the police and EMTs came and she ministered to his burns as she gave him the best whut-fer of all time.

CC and I put our houses up for sale not long after we got married and bought our first place together. Now, you're probably thinking, and I do not blame you for doing so, that we bought some loft in Midtown Atlanta and are living the City Life. In this you would be wrong.

You see, I had a vision for what I wanted to do in the music business, Jazz specifically, in the Metro Atlanta area. CC loved the vision, too. We escaped to the country and found a house well outside the metro area with a huge great room sporting high ceilings and good acoustics, several nicely sized bedrooms, three full bathrooms, big country-style kitchen, and floors suitable for dogs to live in happily. The property also has a barn with stables and workshop. The whole thing sits on sixty acres of rolling hills populated with pine, what we in the South call the first cash crop.

You can guess what the second cash crop is and it ain't peanuts or Vidalia onions, but we don't fool around with any of that funny stuff.

There are fenced-in paddocks for horses to kick up their heels in. The nearest neighbor is at least two miles away and you can't see them because of the trees. Trees make a good sound buffer. County land use codes said farming, business, and residential are all allowed. To top it all off, a small river runs through it.

In other words, we were in the boonies. Perfect.

I felt privileged to be involved in bringing Jazz to the forefront and building on the legacy of those who helped define the art form. So, on this land I saw stables being rented for horse lovers who can't keep one in their subdivisions. Sixty acres for riding is not a bad incentive.

The great room was turned into a studio where I record, produce, and engineer my albums and others. I've started an independent label, as well.

Pine, stable rentals, and other fees bring in cash. Plus, a penny saved is a penny earned, so all in all, the vision is coming together. I can see Jazz Camps for kids and concerts under a large shed-type roof with a big walk-in fireplace. BYOB, of course. I wanted to build a Jazz destination here in Georgia. Laid back. Welcoming. Friendly. Not corporate owned. Tickets sold from my website without all those international ticket bullies getting in the mix.

I think I can do it.

No. I know I can.

I know *we* can.

My best friend, Misha Stefanuk, loves the idea also. He doesn't see himself as a partner, but I do and you just wait and see. I'll get him to be more than just a good buddy helping out a friend.

CC and I started calling it The Farm because its on farms that food is grown to feed the physical souls of billions of people. Our farm would feed folks, too: Heart and soul.

Adman hears about a death

CC's alarm went off early. Okay. It went off at the right time for her, but it was early for me…or would've been if I'd heard it. I did not and slept straight through. On the other hand, CC hears the alarm and jumps up like a racehorse from a gate when a starter gun sounds. She's ready to go. I do not remember her leaving. I woke around eleven to a text tone. Looked at my phone but it was blurry. So I went to the bathroom and splashed cold water on my face until my eyes worked.

Out of habit, I looked at myself in the mirror, but was unable to see all of my face because stuck to the glass were several bright orange Post-it Notes. Seems my CC was enamored of my attentions when I got home from RLC last night and woke her. Oh, the adjectives she used! Why, I'd tell you but you'd be embarrassed…or jealous.

In any case, I was smiling when I walked back to the nightstand and picked up the phone. The text was from Misha. It said —

```
Call me. Barry Lamon's dead. I hear
suicide.
```

Smile vanished. What? Barry's dead? I called Misha. He answered.

"What happened?" I said.

"Jaaahnn," heavy Russian accent front and center. "Barry kee-al heemself. Poison."

"What kind of poison?"

"Do not know."

"Dang. I had no idea he was depressed. Or was he sick and didn't want to die a lingering death?"

"Hmmm…theess eess possible," Misha answered. "Don't know. He found way to make painleees as pohhseeeble."

"How's that?"

"Baked it into cookies."

"What? That's weird. How do they know that?"

"*Vskrytiye trupa*…ummm…oo-toopsee."

"Have you heard about the funeral?"

"Yes. Too late. He die two weeks ago."

"Geez. How is it we are just now hearing about this? I should send the family a card. You know his mailing address?"

"No. I put condolenzz on hees Wall."

"I'll get a mailing address. I'll let you know."

We hung up and I went to the computer, logged onto Facebook, went to his wall, found where a relative posted about his death. I sent a private direct message to the relative and asked for an address to send a card. By the time I finished with a shower an answer arrived with the address. I had to go out and get a few groceries. The list was on the kitchen table. I added condolence card to the bottom of the list, grabbed my car keys, and headed to Publix. The reason I headed to Publix was because I had to get lunch and today lunch was a sub sandwich kind of day. I loved their sub sandwiches.

You may be asking, "Adman, why not just post condolences on his Wall? Why send a card?" For one: I did post condolences. Two: Digital condolences cannot be held in the hand years from now. See how that works? I'd worked with Barry Lamon on several gigs and had always liked him. His family had to be feeling bad about the suicide of their loved one. I wanted to say something nice that would make them remember the good about him. A personal message, written by hand, means much more to those who grieve.

Shopping done and put up, card written, envelope addressed and stamped, I prepared for Dad coming over.

He had completely retired a couple of years ago. Mom kept him busy with some honey-do's around the house. She had said, "John, if he sits down, he'll die. I aim to not let him sit for long. Keep him busy, that's my plan."

I took the hint and, since I had plenty of projects he could help me with, what with my music vision being huge and I couldn't do it alone, then Dad might as well help out, right? Besides that, who could beat free labor? Dad saw Mom's plan even if she thought she was being sneaky about it. "John, your mother's right. If I sit in a chair and wait, I'll die pretty quick."

We didn't want him dead until it was his time, so come on Dad, bring your hammer and your carpentry savvy and let's get to it. And we had. Permits and weather delays and money always calling the shots to our schedule. After a year we had the pole barn up with a roof over it; now we were tricking it out.

Mom came with him tonight and brought all the fixin's for supper. CC loved Mom's cooking. Dad and I left her alone to get it going and we went out to the barn. Four stables were rented with owners responsible for feeding, grooming, mucking, exercising, and taking them from stable to pasture. Our job was to keep the facilities in proper working order, safe, dry, and provide plenty of wheat straw to use in the stalls. It was working out quite well. I liked horses, but I didn't like them well enough to pay that kind of money to keep one.

Horses, while physically powerful, are delicate creatures. Vets that treat large animals know this. Owners quickly find out just how delicate if they are slow on the upkeep. Horses have personalities and quirks, and can have mental health issues, too.

If equines are particularly social and don't get enough mental stimulation, they have been known to chew the wood in their stables. It's called cribbing. Horses in the wild don't chew wood. They don't get bored. Horses kept in unnatural environments do get bored and crib. Splinters and small pieces of wood can pass into the stomach and through the intestine and give them colic, or puncture their intestines. A horse in pain is not a pretty thing to watch...or so the vet told me.

To help with that boredom, several owners brought small but tough rubber balls they can kick around the stall. If you look out into the field, you'll see three giant rubber balls that are filled with air. I love watching them kick and jump over them. You can see how much fun they're having.

Anyway, today Dad and I had to repair a couple of hinges on a stall door and we got busy with that. Then we walked around the barn to the workshop. We had already started working on a rack for the recording studio that would hold cords and other items. We spent the next three hours on it. A vet had come and gone, as had a groomer and an owner. I heard CC drive up and before too long she texted it was time for us to come eat. I locked up the workshop and we went in.

Biscuits and white gravy with sausage. Baked chicken and green beans. Rice, thick-sliced Vidalia onions, and ripe Big Boy tomatoes from Mom's garden with all the salt and pepper my little heart desired. Dang, that was some good eating. Good thing Mom doesn't live here or I'd be fat as a pig just before it was taken to market. CC tucked in with gusto.

She did not know how to cook like this, but wanted to learn. Since her mother had passed away when she was young, CC needed a mother figure. Mom was happy to oblige. Especially if it meant her son wouldn't starve. The first thing she had to do was learn how to prepare the tomato for eating. One must peel it first, then slice. The skin has a bitter bite to it that you don't notice until you eat a *skint 'mater* and then eat one unpeeled. From that point forward, every time you see a sliced tomato with the skin on, you'll just shake your head in disgust and pass the plate to the next person.

Over supper, I told them about Barry Lamon killing himself with poisoned cookies. That was sad, but Mom had some good questions. Why wouldn't he just eat the cookies in between taking the poison in its purest state? And wouldn't the poison be weakened by heat from cooking? Furthermore, she said, how big a batch were the cookies? It would take a lot of poison not to be diminished in strength. How fast did he die? Mom did not believe he killed himself in this fashion.

CC stared at Mom, but Dad and I were used to such from her. She was not a stupid woman, that's for sure. And we tended to believe her in this because she had been a pharmacist for fifteen years. She quit the daily store grind and turned to consulting for the next decade. Then it was time to retire and really ramp up her garden and enjoy the grands that were coming along.

"Mom," I said. "Are you saying he was murdered?"

"No. Then again, maybe. I'm just saying the poison could have been administered another way. Or both ways for good measure, but I doubt very seriously it was accidental."

CC and I looked at each other and shuddered. Was another murder spree starting up again?

A summit is called of the Amateur Sleuth Society

The next day my phone started blowing up with texts from the Amateur Sleuth Society. Mario Alberto Mireles had died. Suicide by poison. All by himself. In his Stone Mountain apartment. Seemed he mixed his poison with peach-flavored vodka. The texts all said the same thing: Not possible that in the Atlanta Jazz community two musicians would kill themselves within two weeks with poison.

The Amateur Sleuth Society was formed a few years back when a Jazz guitarist by the stage name of Reign got mad at a few folks and proceeded to dispatch them with extreme prejudice. He's the one who held me and CC hostage; he's now serving life in prison. Before that happened, though, I had invited a few musicians over to help me try to figure out who was doing this. Reign had sent me anonymous letters so we had a lot of incentive to figure it out. Come to find out, we all knew him.

This time, no letters have arrived, but we'd all come to the same conclusion: The killer of our two friends had to be the same person and we had to know him. I called Mom and told her about the latest death. She said it was a woman. Women use poison. They are very passive-aggressive like that, she said.

Geez. What the heck? I texted the Amateur Sleuth Society to come to my house and we'd have a meeting about it. Maybe we could figure out how to identify the killer. I told them Mom's idea that the killer had to be a female. That freaked them out and I'll tell you why. Men will gladly face down all kinds of danger. We all know that the female is the most dangerous species of all.

Two days later, at lunchtime, I had pizzas ordered and beers ice cold in the fridge. Misha had been out here, of course, as had Ty and Arturo, but the rest of the Amateur Sleuth Society had not. Of course, I gave them a tour. Then the pizza delivery guy showed up with five large pizzas of varying varieties. A couple of the guys grabbed boxes, I paid the driver a good tip before he left, and then we headed inside to eat, drink, and discuss.

Ty, Carl, Arturo, André, David, Chip, Gerry, and Leland all could make it.

Ty was the first to speak. "I'll have a slice of pepperoni and one with everything." He held out a paper plate and two slices were chucked onto it. He dropped the plate to the table in front of him with a sigh and popped the top on a Pabst. Everybody else was all elbows and slurps and burps and it wasn't until after a couple of slices and a beer were downed by each that anybody spoke again.

Gerry said, "I cannot believe that Mario killed himself. It makes no sense. We had plans."

"What plans and when?" David burped out.

"We were going fishing. He loves fishing. I've got a boat and we had a whole day planned starting at four in the morning, uhhhh," Gerry thought, "two Saturdays from now. He wouldn't kill himself." Gerry shook his head no, burping as he reached for another slice.

By the time we finished the pizza and beers, everybody had agreed with Gerry. Then Ty summed it up for all. "Yeah, well…what can we do about it?"

Nobody knew what to do. So, what with gigs and students and shedding to be attended to, the guys left with promises to group text any ideas.

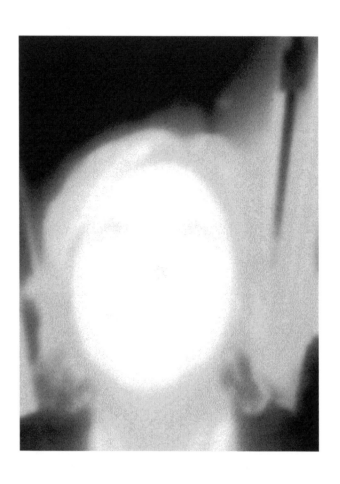

Adman gets tagged and texted

Shave and a haircut, two bits.

Or as written in the C scale: C G-G A-G B-C. Thus ended the Birmingham Jazz Festival Misha and I headlined. Our band was made up of a couple of Young Lions we'd heard several times at both Red Light Café and Après Diem and liked them. They were from B'ham, so they were playing to a home crowd. Cousins, parents, aunties and uncles, school chums, all came out to hear them and cheer them on. One trumpet, one guitar. It was clear they practiced together and the audience were fans, too. Little Man was on drums. Misha on keys, of course.

Misha and I had arrived Friday in our special van. I already had an Econoline van used to haul equipment when on tour here in the Southeast. Then Misha and I raised the top a full eighteen inches and built bunks with storage underneath. We use truck stop showers and don't need television or mini bottles of booze at inflated prices, so we save a lot of money on hotel costs. Plus, that limited female drama, too. I mean, really…where would we take them, right? Misha didn't need any more drama, that's for sure. Divorced three times, and with one kid, he couldn't afford another woman. He wasn't even dating. Not that opportunity didn't come his way, but his goal was to manage their expectations while remaining out of their clutches.

CC is the one who named the vehicle. She was tired of calling it the van, so she started calling it The Van. Like the group of session musicians that ended up calling itself The Band. She even had a license plate made for the front that said The Van and in smaller letters For The Band. It was too funny. You might not think so, but as they say: Guess you had to be there.

We dropped in for meet-and-greets with a few venue owners. Future gig planning. Then the festival was the next day, Saturday. Like I said, it turned out nicely. We were very pleased to be able to help them raise money and raise the Jazz profile. I texted CC that we were heading back to Georgia. Got to The Farm — hey, I'm seeing a trend — where Misha climbed in his car and drove home. I pulled The Van into the attached garage. Dad and I had raised the entryway to accommodate the high roof. Sure was nice having a retired father.

CC heard me pull in and met me at the mudroom next to the garage. I pushed the button to close the roll-up door, stepped inside, and gave my woman a big ol' hug. It was late, I was hungry, and she had a sandwich and beer waiting on me.

"Misha didn't want to stay for a snack?" she asked.

"Nah," I mumbled through sliced ham, pickles, and sourdough with cheese. I swallowed. "He said to tell you hello, but he wanted to get to his own bed." I ripped off another chunk of sandwich.

"How'd it go?"

I chewed faster and swallowed again. Chased it with a sip of beer. "Great. Got a few pictures." I slid my phone out of my pocket and she flipped through the album.

"Looks like a lot of fun. Glad it went good."

She plugged the charger to the phone, hit the Dropbox upload button, and the photo album updated to The Cloud...hahaha...I mean, the cloud. Sandwich and beer finished, we went to bed.

On Sunday I logged onto Facebook to update my marketing and found I'd been tagged in three different posts. It was Roxanne Robards who tagged me. Seems the other week when we played together at Skywalker's jam at RLC, somebody had taken several short videos with her phone. She was just now getting around to uploading them. She tagged Ty, Little Man, Skywalker, Michael, Ellen, and RLC, too. The girl understood marketing, that's for sure, because she wrote a short but snappy recap of the evening, but since I've already told you about it, there's no need repeating it here. I clicked "Add to Timeline" and Loved the post as well. Then I made a comment about how much I enjoyed that evening and tagged Ruby Grace since it was her song.

I uploaded the festival pictures and tagged everybody in the band, plus the festival and organizers, too. That done I set my mind to thinking about the killer. I had a sinking feeling that we were somehow connected. Not that the thought was far from the realm of possibility. I knew the two victims. The Jazz community was small. My summary came in 5/4 time —

1 Ergo
2 ipso
3 de facto
4 boom-boom
5 connection!

I played around with that in my head for awhile to see if it could make a fun song. I wrote it on a Post-it Note and stuck it on the computer screen frame.

Mom had said it takes a special kind of woman to kill by poison. They are usually quite feminine and seem so innocent and helpful and warm and nobody ever suspects them…even their victims don't. They have a core of steel that remains frozen, unthawed; plus, they want what they want. Psychopaths. Sociopaths. Or, as Mom said, just plain evil with a can of salted nuts to boot. Somebody never to take for granted. They come in all shapes, sizes, and flavors.

Who did I know like that? We creatives are a weird bunch anyway. Some of us dance along the sharp edge of crazy. Ain't calling any names here. Still, that didn't mean bad intent. How do you identify bad intent when it is hidden? I couldn't. Reading minds is not my gift.

Over the next few days I let all that percolate in the back of my brain. Lots of projects were always cooking at my place and in my head. Figuring out a killer was just another day in Adman Land.

Ruby came over Monday, middle of the day, to work on songs. We were thinking of doing a series of small shows together featuring her originals and mine plus what we wrote together. We'd try the songs on paying audiences. See which ones worked and which needed tweaking. Maybe tempo changes. Chord refinements. Style alterations. Then we would pick the best and do an album. The whole project could take two years or more.

Sounds like a long time, and maybe it is. But she was married with children and I had a busy schedule, too. Our time was not solely our own. Factor in Misha's schedule and you can see how the timetable could become a nightmare. We were three highly disciplined professionals and we'd make it happen because we never took our eyes off the ball.

Some of those shows could be held in my new performance shed. Dad and I had been working on the sound system, large stage, lighting, and fans to circulate air. Slowly but surely. As budget allowed and as I could scrounge materials and labor.

Everything needed to be weatherproofed. I wanted all electricals and audio to plug directly into outlets that were accessible by flipping lids. That way we wouldn't have to worry about having enough electrical and instrument connections, or worry they were safely grounded, no matter what the weather or the band was. Yes, we could expand past Jazz stylings to — gasp — Rock 'n' Roll or Country/Americana or Big Band.

CC thought it would be smart to do BYOB & BF & CB — otherwise known as Bring Your Own Bottle and Basket of Food and Chairs/Blanket, too. That would keep our costs down, everybody would have what they wanted. We'd provide big trashcans and free parking. Staff overhead would be small. What wasn't to love?

Then I had an even better idea. I could host a two-hour Jazz Jam once every couple of months… Sunday…late afternoon. Free for all, BYOB&BF&CB, but the only ones to play or sing would be students, no professionals. College, high school, middle school, and private students both adult and children. Whoever showed up played or sang with whoever showed up. No prima donnas or primo uomos. Check the ego at the door.

Everybody brings their own instrument(s), invites their own audiences. Then they could make their own show. Decide what to play. Get comfortable on a stage. Make mistakes and go with them. Interact with the audience as they improvise and collaborate on the fly. Try original songs. Two hours; what happens is what happens.

Hmmm…seemed a big undertaking. Maybe every other month wasn't enough? I would have to think about that. And since we are way-way OTP, that probably meant those ITP might not make it regularly.

You want to know what OTP and ITP are? I will explain. You see, around the Metro Atlanta area is a ring road, 285, that we call the Perimeter. You either live ITP, inside the perimeter, or OTP, outside the perimeter. Those who live ITP hate going OTP and vice versa. And for good reasons. Take it from me. I've lived both ITP and OTP and know of what I speak.

I remember growing up OTP, of which Sharpsburg is very much, and I remember having this need for Jazz but there wasn't much of that around me. Yet there I was, where Jazz was not typically taught, played, or listened to, trying to find my people as it were. And now, here I am, living very much OTP again. Knowing there are plenty of students — heck, I bet even music teachers — out here in the boonies who would love to add Jazz into the mix but do not have the opportunity because Jazz is very much ITP and that's just too far to go on a regular basis.

Still, nothing ventured, nothing gained.

To get the word out, I should host a BYOB&BF&CB for the Jazz community and call it the "Adman Needs His New Performance Shed Tested Jam". Then, while everybody is trying out the new stage and connections, I could casually drop overt hints about donated labor in exchange for free beer should anyone want to help with the cause on an ongoing basis.

Incoming text interrupted my reverie —

    Hey adman this is Roxanne Robards
    tagged U on Facebook if U can use footage I
    can email it to u whenever hadd blast let's
    do it again

    Send email addy

I replied —

I saw it. Shared and liked. Thank you.

If you want to, send footage. Can't
guarantee will use.

bookingadman@gmail.com

She replied: its all good.

That was so nice of her.
Gosh.

A rehearsal, a business lesson, and a funeral

It had been almost one week since we had returned from the B'ham Jazz Fest. Misha was expecting me at ten-thirty today, a Friday. We had a couple of new songs we were working on. I had lyrics for a singer plus melody and chord progressions. Misha was working on musical transitions between verses, solos, bridge, etc.

Clutch, a mongrel who adopted Misha a few years ago, met me at the door. He flipped over to his back, legs up in the air, tail wagging, and got a *Whoozagootboy-Yuuzagootboy* and a tummy scratch from me. He followed adoringly up the stairs to Misha's studio, which was in what most folks would call the living room, where sat on one wall a grand piano and on the other a huge organ he built himself, and recording and sound equipment, music stands, wires, and cables and all that stuff. That's right. Misha did not have a wife whining about her precious living room. Just kidding. Women are awesome…most of them. Misha is a professional at what he does. Just like me. We are working musicians as well as, don't ever doubt it, *artistes.*

Which is simply another way of saying decorations, fluffy pillows, and feng shui aren't high on our list of important things. These things don't feed our soul. But recording equipment and mic stands and plug-ins and computers, all seemingly piled around in a random fashion…oh-boy-oh-boy-oh-boy…makes our hearts beat a fast tattoo. Some of y'all know what I'm talking about. And those folks agree. Yes, you do.

Clutch doesn't care what we are or how we decorate. He just loves his belly scratched.

"Jaaahhnn. Are you going to Mario's funeral?"

"When is it?"

"Sunday. Two-thirty. In Marietta."

"Two days from now?"

He nodded. I consulted my calendar. "I'm free. Are you going?" He nodded again. I put it on my calendar. "Where?"

"I text you." And ding went my phone with the address and funeral home name. All that done, we got busy with working out the musical logistics for a song we'd be adding to our performance repertoire.

You've seen cartoons where a particular job is broken down like this: What my boss thinks I do. What my wife thinks I do. What my parents think I do. What other groups think I do. What I really do.

Of course, anybody doing the job depicted always gets a good laugh when it gets to What I Really Do because it is never as exciting or romantic or profitable as everybody else believes it to be.

That's another way of saying that reality doesn't exist until it is experienced firsthand.

Same with being a creative who performs live in front of an audience. The audience may see the lights shining on the sweaty, emoting faces of the people they've paid to see. What they don't see is the effort put forth to bring that show to life. All of the unpaid hours of creating, rehearsing, driving, equipment, repairs, vehicle expense, food, and — you'll love this — intellectual property ownership paperwork that we only hope to be able to turn around and make a living from by selling The Show or merch such as T-shirts and CDs and vinyl and downloads, plus, if we are fortunate, licensing the song to a popular TV show or movie with a long tail.

And do not get me started on streaming income. That's a laugh. The public may be awestruck that an album or song is available for streaming or download from the hot Big Tech Service O' da Year, but bank accounts aren't impressed. We may see a few pennies, but we don't depend upon those to pay the bills. I look at streaming as a loss leader. Advertising that helps people want to come out and see the show and buy my merch.

Protecting and defending intellectual property rights is a huge deal and keeping track of the details takes a lot of effort. Effort most creatives are not willing to take. I never liked the idea of spitting into the wind, so I've always taken care of my IP house. I've got spreadsheets that impress, let me tell you. Song title, lyrics, assigned ISRC (upon release), publishing company, writer, composer and all split sheet details, anyone who is on the song as a work-for-hire, album name (if released on album), performing rights organization assigned to rights holders, album release date, and more. Plus I keep all the handwritten notes for these in their separate large manila envelopes along with hard copies of signed contracts for work for hire and split sheets for other rights holders.

Fans never have to think about any of that. If I ever had to prove I owned a song, I could dang well defend my intellectual property rights in a court of law...and win. Most creatives don't do that and thus they are giving away earning potential. The music business is hard enough without working for free.

Whew! Enough of my preaching.

So that was Friday. Saturday morning Dad came over and we worked on the performance shed until one. I ate lunch, took a shower, got dressed, and from three to six I had a gig at a hotel lobby in Downtown Atlanta and a gig from seven-thirty to ten-thirty at a different hotel banquet room for a meeting of chiropractors. Speeches during dinner, then jokes from the emcee. The crowd loved the rimshots when the punchlines were delivered by the emcee who — please pardon me — "cracked" a lot of jokes that kept the band laughing, too. Then the band cut loose. A small dance floor held a few brave couples. Then we schlepped our gear out to vehicles and on home.

Sunday morning was time to sleep in. CC said she would be happy to go with me to the funeral of one of our Jazz family regulars, dear Mario Mireles. She thought the family would like that. So, after a late breakfast, we dressed for a funeral, and headed to Marietta.

When I was a boy, and funerals had to be attended, I was always complaining. Mom would quote scripture at me. She'd say, "Better to go to the house of mourning than to the house of mirth." Then she'd straighten my tie and, while I attempted to duck, stilled my head as she held my jaw in a vise-like grip with her left hand and licked fingers on her right to swipe at a cowlick.

I did not understand these houses she was talking about. When I was thirty I asked her to explain what she meant. I was beginning to get an inkling, but wanted to know her thoughts.

She said, "Son, a meaningful life isn't mindless partying and joking all the time. Clubs and getting drunk and being entertained — you know, the house of mirth — are not where or when we think deeply about our lives. They offer distraction and relaxation...of sorts...

"But when we go to the house of mourning, a funeral...ah, Son, we contemplate the path we are on. We do the math and we think how many more years we have. We ask what we will do with those. And will we benefit family, friends, society, ourselves, or will what we do hurt them? In other words, John, will folks cry when we die because they will miss us...or will they cry because they are relieved we are gone?"

And so today CC and I went to the house of mourning.

Mario Alberto Mireles was a music teacher at a private school. He was also a trumpet player and a go-to guy for when a trumpet was needed for a gig. He was reliable and generous and his students loved him. Bandleaders could count on him. He would be missed in the good way.

We arrived at the funeral home and found the lot full. So we parked across the street on the side parking lot of a CVS store. Kids and their parents were everywhere. School staff, students, band leaders, several musicians I knew, along with Mario's family filled the chapel at the funeral home.

Mario's last public appearances were SRO at the chapel and the graveside service.

I stood in the sun at the back of the crowd watching everybody, but especially the people I knew. They were thinking. Asking themselves about their lives and the value they brought to the world. I put my arm around CC because she was crying right along with the bawling students. Somebody passed around extra tissues; the box didn't last long. Lastly, we stood in line to shake the hands of and say kind words to Mario's relatives seated in the front row on the velvet covered chairs.

Mom was right.

Better to go to the house of mourning.

And the beat goes on...

I thought about Barry Lamon and Mario Mireles. Positive they were murdered but knowing tying the two would be a longshot. Ty, Arturo, André, Leland, and Gerry, members of the Amateur Sleuth Society, had also been at the funeral and graveside service, after which we walked back to our cars together. Everybody had said hello to CC, but she was still upset and got in the car to finish having a good cry.

Me and the guys stood around talking about what somebody was already calling our Second Case. Other than being in the Jazz community here in Atlanta, we couldn't see anything that would make Barry and Mario targets.

Then Roxanne Robards joined us. She gave hugs to some of the guys and fist-bumped others. "Hey, guys. What's up? You look like you just lost somebody you loved."

Ty said, "Roxanne...we did. This is his funeral."

"Oh. Yeah. I knew that. Bad joke," she said. "Really, y'all look so serious. Whatcha talking about?"

Arturo said, "We think Barry and Mario were murdered. We just can't seem to figure out how or why."

Roxanne looked shocked. "Murdered? Wh-wh-what makes you say that?"

André piped up. "Within what…two weeks? Two Jazz musicians kill themselves by using poison?"

We were all shaking our heads; such a thing simply couldn't happen, yet it did.

"Surely that's possible," Roxanne said.

I said, "Okay, is it possible? Yes. But is it probable? No way in heck."

Roxanne stood there with her mouth flopped open like she wanted to say something but just couldn't. I asked if she was okay.

She found her voice. "Yeah. I'm fine. I just think you guys are making something out of nothing. There is no way anybody would kill Jazz people. I mean rock-and-rollers? Yeah. And country singers? Definitely. But Jazz people? No way. No how."

We all laughed at that.

"What's so funny?" she demanded.

I said, "Roxanne, you've only been in Atlanta now for, what, two and a half years or so?"

She nodded.

"Then you haven't heard about the serial killer."

Leland said, "Spree killer."

We all looked at him like *What's the diff?*

Leland explained. "See, a spree killer kills more than one, thus making a series, but does it in a shorter period of time with no emotional cooling off between murders. A serial killer cools off between his kills."

"Or her kills," Ty said.

Leland nodded. "Or hers."

Roxanne listened intently, as if fascinated and horrified at the same time.

Chip said, "I did not know that."

Leland said, "Yeah, my girlfriend is studying up on that. You know, trying to become a detective."

"Wow," I said on behalf of everybody, then turned back to Roxanne. "Ro-Ro, you haven't heard about the 'spree' killer who killed three Jazz Cats and one Jazz Kitten a few years ago, have you?"

Roxanne shook her head. "I don't know what to say. Why did she kill those people?"

"It wasn't a she. It was a he. And he did it because they each dissed him."

"So he committed murder because he got his panties in a twist? His ego was hurt?" she said. We laughed at that, but nodded our heads. "Nobody is gonna kill for that. They might kill cuz somebody stole something, though, but getting dissed? I think you're all full of it."

Gerry quietly let fly with his favorite expletive, the F-bomb, then said to her, "We aren't full of it. In fact, since Mario's murder, I've been thinking there are going to be more victims. Adman's mom made the case for the murderer being —"

I interrupted quickly. "Hey-hey-hey, there, Gerry. Let's save all that for our next summit."

Roxanne said, "Summit? What summit?"

I laughed it off, "We guys get together every now and then for beers and pizza and just call it a summit. Just us having our little bit o' fun."

"Yeah, but…" Then she put on her best man-eating smile and looked around from one to another. "Can I come?"

Everybody's eyes got big and they lost their tongues, then turned to me. I put my arm around Roxanne's shoulders and said, "Nope. Boys only. Hey, we pass gas and groom our noses — and burp after quaffin' beer —"

"Groom noses? Quaffin'?" she said.

"Groom. A/K/A pickin'. Quaffin' means slurpin', sluggin', guzzlin'…" Still no understanding in her eyes, so I tried one more. "Drankin'?"

"Pickin' and drankin'?"

"That's right. You aren't from the South. Let me translate. Drankin' means drink*ing*."

"Oh. You are funny, Adman." She smiled in such a way I thought good thing CC was in the car crying and not watching this man-eater in action at a funeral. Still, there was something else in her eyes. Couldn't quite name it, but I didn't like it.

Oh, well. Enunciating my gerunds clearly, I continued to explain. "So, after much beer drink*ing* and scarf*ing* of pizza — trust me on this, a delicate flower such as yourself does not want to be in same room when we have our boys club."

She shuddered and said, "Ewww."

Yeah. We all got a good laugh when she said that. I thought I might want to change the subject and so I did. "Hey, while I got all you here, I'm thinking about putting on a Jam to test out my new performance shed. You know…give the sound system and everything a really good workout. Y'all wanna come?"

Roxanne said, "Me, too?"

"Absolutely. This will be open to anybody. Bring your friends to listen or play. We want to give it a great tryout. Ruby Grace must come, of course. Her husband and kids could come out, too. In fact, you know what? I should tell everybody with kids to bring them so they can play on The Farm. Heck, bring picnic stuff and all that. Give the whole shebang a real-world workout, right?"

Everybody thought that was a grand idea and right that second sent an email note to self to pick a day and send notifications out. We said goodbye and parted. I walked to the car where CC now had herself calmed down.

"Baby," she sniffled. "I am so sorry I couldn't stay up there with y'all. This funeral just brought back all the sadness from my parents' deaths. I needed to cry."

I put the key in the ignition, started the car, and left the graveyard, I mean, the memorial garden. We headed home, sad still.

Yet even now, thinking about it later, it was a far better thing to go the house of mourning that day — and for more than one reason.

Hit the ground running

When CC and I got home we were worn out. A nap was in order. We fell asleep quickly…well, I did for sure. Woke myself up with a loud snore that, for once, did not make it to CC's consciousness. I rolled over and proceeded to sleep some more. We woke, refreshed. I looked at the clock and was surprised to see it was so late.

"Babe, it's ten o'clock. I'm hungry." To make my point, I slapped my belly. "Hear the echo of emptiness?"

She rolled off the bed to a standing position and stretched like a cat. "Come on then. Let's go make some supper. You pour the wine."

From the fridge, CC pulled the makings for sandwiches and opened a bag of salt and vinegar chips. I got the corkscrew from the drawer and hauled a bottle of Merlot from the pantry shelf to the table and thus, with the sounds of domestic harmony clanking throughout the kitchen, in no time at all the table was set, sandwiches built, chips crunched, and wine quaffed until bellies were full and we again quietly answered the siren call of sleep and hopefully sweet dreams.

Thus ended Sunday. Come Monday, we hit the ground running. CC drove to work. As for me, first the shed's performance rehearsal must be scheduled. Grabbing a pen and pad of paper, phone in pocket, I walked out the door.

The way our property is laid out, you come in off the main road onto a long driveway. To the left and right of the drive begins our cash crop, pine trees. Meander for a bit until you come to a large clearing on the left between the river and the pines. Passing that, you'll come to a bridge that crosses the river and on up to a smaller drive to the house on the right. Keep following the larger driveway to get to barn and paddocks.

You know what, let me draw it out for you.

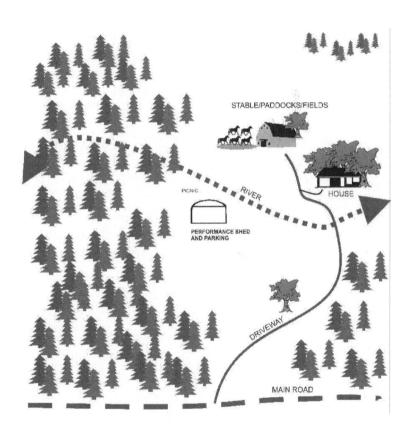

As you can see, until we get another bridge built across the river, I had to walk the long way around. Still, no formal drive to the shed. And, dang it, no signage pointing the way. I wrote that down. Then I got to thinking about the picnic area. Sure, folks would like to spread their blankets under the shed, but overflow? Should it be sodded or should we just spread a bunch of wheat straw? Straw was cheaper. Straw it is. Under the shed's shade I sat on the ground and immediately had another to-do item: Rocks. The ground needed a good going over with a short-tined rake to find any rocks that could cause a body to be uncomfortable. Adding another item to the list, I heard a vehicle coming up the driveway. Sounded like Misha's car and it was.

Climbing out, he shut the car door. Standing akimbo, he looked the shed over and up and down. "Jaaahnnn! Eeess lookin' goot," he hollered, then walked over and took a seat on the ground beside me. "Ow! Eees rock." He moved around until he was free of it. "Whaasssss oop?"

"Just making a list and checking it twice."

"Eees not Chreeesmus. Lehmesee." I handed him the pad and he read it. "Rocks? Wheat straw? Signage? Nothing else?"

"I just got here, Misha. Give me time, man."

"You wann check electroocul and sond?"

"Yeah. And all those big overhead fans."

"And zah lighz, too."

We got up and walked to the switch panel. Each fan had its own switch, as did each light. Stage lights were not included in this panel. Those were in the sound booth. Fans and overhead lights worked. Outside lighting worked. Misha went to his car and got his keyboard. With me carrying it from outlet to outlet, Misha plugged it into each and switched the power on. All those worked just fine.

Now for the sound test. Oops. Another item for the list: Electrical extension cords or built-in plugs? If cords, we'd need several rated for outdoor use. I'm thinking power strips all the way around the stage. The one cord that was there got plugged into the stage power panel.

More for the list: Direct inputs and cables and connectors, and a place to house and secure those when we weren't there. Misha had one long audio cord in his car. While he went to get it, I unlocked the sound booth. Next thing you know music was ringing out. Four horses' heads popped up from grass and they came trotting over to the fence line. I laughed.

"Hey, Misha. We got us some fans." I pointed back over his shoulder. "At least we know how far the sound carries."

Misha turned to look and laughed, too, then began playing "Mi Caballo Blanco". Set in the Andes mountains of South America, it was a Chilean folk song that was so old the composer was listed as "Chilean Folk Song". Misha's fingers were smoking this morning. Thus inspired, and having learned the song in Spanish class in high school, it was only natural I would sing along. Next thing you know, I'm prancing around like I'm riding my white horse and belting out the lyrics.

Es mi caballo blanco,
como un amanecer
Siempre juntitos vamos,
es mi amigo más fiel.
Mi caballo, mi caballo,
galopando va,
Mi caballo, mi caballo,
se va y se va.
En alas de una dicha
mi caballo corrió
Y en brazos de una pena
también él me llevó.
Mi caballo, mi caballo,
galopando va,
Mi caballo, mi caballo,
se va y se va.

By the time the last notes rang out, three horses had already gone back to grazing, but one was feeling the joy with us and was out in the field kicking a big ball around in time to the music. I swear. When we finished, he was throwing his head around then staring at us like "Wait. Whut? Don't stop? We're just getting started with the party!" Oh where, oh where is a videographer when you need one? Can you say Viral YouTube Comedy Hit?

Though I can sing, I am not a singer and do not sing on stage in front of audiences. It's not my thang. I'm not that good. Now, if you need a singer to inject humor into a dull set, hey, I'm all over that. In any case, we checked out all the sound system, including the sound board, as best we could. More for the list: Mics (vocal and instrument), mic stands, instrument stands.

"Hey, Misha. Want to stay for lunch? I've got sandwich makings."

"Hell, yes. What ees sanwhish 'makings'?"

"Meat. Cheese. Lettuce. Bread. Pickles. Mayo. Mustard…makings."

"Ah. Yes. Stoof you 'make' sanwhish with."

"You're catching on quick."

"Jaaahnn. When you build bridge, I help. K?"

"I will not turn down free labor, my friend."

He put his keyboard in the backseat, and gave me a ride up to the house.

Figuring and planning

There comes a time in every business owner's life — and that is what I am, a business owner — when you see money going out and the equivalent not coming in and you ask "What the heck am I doing?" But you have to keep believing in yourself, your vision, and just spend the money and pray and hope — and work and work toward your goals. Or, what we in the South call it: Stepping into it hard.

Before Dad and I could build a secure and insulated box for mics and stands and such, I had to know how many I'd need. So after Misha left when lunch was finished, I walked back down and began imagining stage setups. I took Sweet Stella with me.

How many singers would be up at any one time? How many horns would be playing and would they all need to be mic'd? In other words, a Big Band setup with all those horns would probably not need mic'ing, but one to five horns might. Drums might need to be mic'd, too. All of that would need to be weighed against the crowd size as bodies tend to soak up sound. More bodies, more enhancement of sound needed so that those in the back could hear just as well.

I got my configuring done and notes made, then opened up Stella's case and proceeded to blow for about thirty minutes. With nothing in the way to impede them, Stella's sweet sounds bounced around the wide open spaces and echoed back at me. I felt better and Stella and I walked back home in a leisurely fashion.

I checked my phone and saw two texts. One was from Dad:

`Bright idea. Coming over to explain.`

The other from Roxanne:

`can I come see that shed thing?`

I thought, you know, I don't want to be alone with Ro-Ro because she's just too flirty and the one thing I don't need is any woman drama. So

`Sure. Saturday morning around nine would be best.`

I sent her the address then texted CC that I would need her to be around Saturday morning and walk to the shed with me and Roxanne so I could show her around. CC replied

`Smart man. Love you.`

Dad pulled up not long after. I hopped in his car and we drove to the shed.

"Okay, son. Here's my idea. Why can't we build an overhead track system that will move microphones around?"

"Hey, Dad. Love the idea, but you do realize I'm not made of money, right?"

He laughed but proceeded to explain. "Wouldn't cost much. And I am donating my labor." We stared up at the rafters of the roof. "Son, see, I figured — and you correct me if I'm wrong — but I figured every act has a center. So," he pointed, "here's the center of the stage. We have a sound setup here. Duplicate that two more times, one on either side, so that when a band expands, we've got what we need."

I thought about that and said, "That would help with Big Bands, too. Mics are lowered and hung above their heads. Drums could be easily mic'd."

"Drums need mic'ing?"

"Definitely. Especially when played in large areas. We need to think about this. Let's not start on that quite yet. Instead, why don't you be out here the day we do our first Test Jam."

"Yeah, sure. That would work."

Then we got busy designing a built-in equipment storage area. Again Dad had a question.

"John, why do you want a cabinet? Isn't that like advertising where you keep all your stuff?"

"What do you have in mind?"

"Under the stage there is a lot of wasted space. So, my idea is to have a series of drawers —"

"You mean, a skinny ones for mics and for DIs and for cords? And a larger one for mic stands and music stands?"

"Yes, exactly. Each can be locked. All have the added protection from the weather by the floor of the stage, and they are hidden away. When the sound booth thing here is locked up, it just looks like a table at the side because of how it folds out. A locked cabinet would have to be huge and would look messy, too."

"Dad, you are one fart smella." We laughed at my favorite childhood joke for smart fella. It had been quite a while since I'd used it. "Hey, Dad. You remember that time you got called to the school because I called the principal a fart smella?" We laughed some more. Yeah, that was a fond fifth-grade memory.

"Yeah, yeah, yeah. And you remember we're sitting in the principal's office and he's all mad and I don't know what this is about and then he tells me and I started laughing because it was so funny?"

We doubled over laughing and slapped our legs and clutched at our chests gasping for breath and horses were staring at us wanting in on the fun. We staggered to the car and fell in. Dad finally got himself under control enough so he could find the slot for the car key and we drove back to the house to design the equipment drawers.

I told Dad to stop for a minute and rolled my window down because I saw a hawk sitting on a wire and wanted to get a picture of it. That done, we continued to the house where we were still busy with designing the drawers when CC got home.

"Hey, babe," I said, giving her a kiss and a hug.

With my arms still wrapped around her, she spoke over my shoulder, "Hey, Dad. What'chall working on?"

"You are gonna love this," Dad said. "Storage drawers that go under the stage. Holds mics, stands, DIs — whatever those are —"

I interrupted. "Direct inputs."

"Again, whatever those are," he continued. "And cords and cables. Protected from the weather and better hidden from the opportunistic thief."

"Sounds great. You ought to have them set back into the stage and a hangy down flappy thingy to hide the locked drawers, too."

Dad and I looked at each other. "Now that's good idea," he said. "I'm gonna go on home. Work on this later. When you gonna have that run-thru?"

"I'll let you know."

He hugged CC and me and out he went. At which point I turned to CC and planted a big fat one on her lips and backed her up to the counter and got a little frisky with her. Yeah, I can still make her eyes glaze over. Then she proceeded to show me who was boss and thusly it was a little while later when we got around to preparing the evening meal.

One busy week begins...

That was Monday. Come Tuesday it was time for me and Misha to do some shedding and I was over at his place bright and early — in musician time, that is. Misha made coffee and stared at me bleary-eyed over his cup.

"Whaaat zee matter weesh you?" I asked, imitating his accent.

He gave me a *that's not funny* look and mumbled. "In*soam*neeah."

"Why?" I asked and sat at the kitchen table.

He made a rotating motion around his head with his left index finger.

"Oh. Her."

He nodded. You see, when The Muse has something to say, she doesn't care that you will die in order to give her a listen. She is a tough mistress from which true creatives cannot escape and spoke quite often to Misha — and insistently. Though she did come and go in phases, she was coming on hard to him right now. Creatives might complain about the side effects of The Muse, but never about The Muse herself.

The Muse feeds and animates our souls. And when we output her vision, filtered through our senses and sensibilities, the rest of the world is fed. It is a great responsibility and one real creatives do not take lightly.

"Yes. Her." Misha swigged the last of his coffee and off we went to his living room studio to work on our craft. While we had just come off from headlining the Jazz Festival in Birmingham a couple of weeks ago or so, we had another Southeast tour coming up in a few weeks. As busy as we both were, if we didn't carve out the time to work on our show, we wouldn't be getting any more gigs…and that's a fact. Three hours later I'm heading home with the firm commitment to pick a Test Jam date and push the word out when I got there.

I made myself a snack and got a beer and took a look at my calendar. Two things had to be fitted in: A meeting of the Amateur Sleuth Society and the Test Jam. Test Jam I set for the third Saturday morning from now. To announce it, I posted on social media then emailed all on my list of musicians, drummers, singers, and didgeridoo players that I knew. Laid out the parameters and the goal. Gave the address. Hey, whoever showed up showed up.

Next I set a date for the Amateur Sleuth Society this coming Thursday around lunch, two days from now. Sent text to Ty, Carl, Arturo, André, David, Chip, Misha, Gerry, and Leland. Beer and pizza, too,

I told them. Ty said he had a student and David and Gerry said they were out of town. The rest were good to go. Sweet! More pizza for me. What am I saying? More beer for me.

I also sent a text to Roxanne Robards confirming Saturday morning. She replied in the affirmative. I looked at the clock. CC would be home before too long. We'd do dinner and visit for awhile, then I thought I'd go to Joe's Jazz Jam. It had been awhile since I'd seen ol' Joe. We were both very busy working musicians with a few private students. Joe was a good guy. He was the quintessential mentor of the Jazz community, not only here in Atlanta, but the broader community, too. I missed him.

I took a nap and next thing I know CC was shaking my shoulder. "John? Wake up, you. What ya want for supper?"

I forced my eyes open and looked at the clock. "Mmmm...hey, you hot mama you." She smiled and gave my butt a loving slap. She left for the kitchen. In a rolling stretch I jumped out of bed to join her.

Holding the fridge door for her I said, "How was your day?"

"Great. Busy. Aggravating. You know, normal."

She handed me one mysterious bowl after another to put on the counter. *Whoozagootboy? Youzaagootboy! Yes. You. Are.* "What's all this, honey bunch?"

"Tonight is leftover night," she said and pulled out three more bowls. I closed the fridge.

"I see Mama done taught you her trick."

"Yes, she did. I think I will rename it to Supper Surprise Night."

"I like it."

And with that we got busy reheating several days worth of leftovers. We had a feast and then cleaned the kitchen. I got dressed, kissed CC, and me and Sweet Stella were out the door at nine o'clock. We would make it to Joe's around nine-thirty or so, depending on whether highways were clear of accidents.

Now, some of you are wondering why CC doesn't go with me but only occasionally. For the same reason I don't go with her to her place of work. Jams may look like "fun", and they are for fans, but they're work for us. Yes, boys and girls, it is work entertaining folks. It is work standing on a stage and smiling. Massive amounts of energy are poured out. Jams are easier on singers and musicians who randomly show up, but networking with others in the Jazz community is also work. CC doesn't take me into her meetings. See how it works?

And so Stella and I made it closer to nine fifty because I forgot the gas tank was almost empty and a fill-up was necessary and I got to craving a Snickers bar, so an inside visit to the QuikTrip was absolutely necessary. But make it we finally did. The venue was packed tonight, which meant parking this late was at least two blocks away. I grabbed Stella and slung her over my back, locked the doors, and started walking. Random notes came floating over the air. The closer I got the less random those notes were until I could see the band was going crazy over "Spain" by Armando Anthony "Chick" Corea, a Jazz pianist/electric keyboardist and composer, sadly now dead. Composed in 1971, the original and most well-known version is on the album *Light as a Feather*. Corea played a Rhodes electric piano, Airto Moreira was on drums, Flora Purim with vocals and percussion, Stanley Clarke on his bass, and Joe Farrell on flute.

Like all songs that become standards, there is no one definitive version any longer. Especially when playing live. The reasons for that are many and would take too long to explain, but I can sum it up: Live entertainment is always fluid. Even with the same people playing the same songs, no two live shows will be the same. In live shows, especially Jazz, moods rule. Anger, happiness, jealousy, petty disagreements, opinion, and other passions of those on stage are played out in the moment. That's why live Jazz is never as good once it is recorded. There's an essential physical vibe in the air moving around and between performers and audience that does not make it when recorded in bits and bytes.

In plain fact, you actually have to be there in the same room to experience the full effect. I know the song by the Atlanta Rhythm Section says imaginary lovers never let you down, but everybody's always looking to be touched by another for real. Many songs bemoan the lack of touch or of it leaving. Even bad love is better than no love at all.

And why is that? Because there is no substitute for live and in person.

Thus, tonight, I heard yet another version of "Spain" — one that would never be played again — as it reverberated through the window I watched through behind the busy and packed bar. There was Joe, making nice with old fans and welcoming new ones into the family. Ty was on keys. Boxx on bass.

David on drums. Couple of young players on horns sweating bullets to keep up. Pops on guitar.

I went to the door and walked in. Joe smiled and came over with his famous fist bump. To be more accurate, it wasn't famous, but it was definitely unique in the delivery. He had this way of all at once grinning, cocking his head, pulling up his shoulders, and twisting his body as he moved toward you holding out a fist.

"Adman. Where you been, brutha?"

"Busy as heck, that's where."

"How's CC?"

"Just fine. Did you get my email about the performance shed Test Jam?"

"Yeah, man. I did. Hey, gotta go introduce some new folks. We'll talk about it later tonight, yeah?"

I nodded but Joe was walking away, blowing his horn with the band to end the performance. He hopped up on stage and got applause for everybody up there and then called up the next group. Ty saw me and waved, as did David and Boxx. Pops was coming off the stage and passed me on the way to his seat.

"Hey, Adman. Where you been hiding?"

"Working on a bunch of stuff, bro." I walked with him to his case and watched him wipe the sweat off his guitar and pack it up carefully. "Did you get my email about the Test Jam for the performance shed?"

"Yeah, I did. Can I bring some of my students?"

"Sure. That would be great. Make sure they bring water and food if they need it as we are not set up for service."

"Will do. See you then."

"And Adman is here tonight, too. Hey, Adman!" This was Joe from the stage. "I see Sweet Stella. You playing tonight?"

I held a hand up in the air and said, "Heck, yeah."

"Sweet. We'll get him up in a little bit, folks."

With that, the band was kicking it again. This time, Ruby Grace was on the stage. She gave me a little waggle of her fingers to say hello and off she went singing "I Can't Seem to Cry [Over You]". Yeah, she wrote that song. The lyrics were simple, but the way she sang it gave it its sadness.

Verses 1 and 2:
[Slow and sad and rubato]
I cry over puppies
I cry over kittens
I even cry over spilt milk
But no matter
How hard I try
I can't seem to cry over
[at tempo] you

I cry when my groceries
Are bagged upside down
I even cry over burnt toast
But no matter
How hard I try
I can't seem to cry over you

Bridge: *[Up tempo bossa]*
Cross my heart and
Hope to die

Stick a needle
In my eye
If I lie
Yes, no matter
How hard I try
[Slow tempo again]
I can't seem to cry over you

[Solos for musicians, leading back to the Bridge]

Outro: *[Rubato]*
I cry over puppies
I cry over kittens
I even cry…
over…
over…
…you

As I knew they would, the audience loved it. Joe said, "Ruby Grace, everyone. Ruby, you wrote this song, didn't you?" Ruby nodded. The audience went *aaahhh*. "Dang, woman. You just about made me cry." She left the stage with a little bow and a hug for Joe. And now I was up. "Adman! Come on up, my friend."

Ruby hugged me when we passed and next thing I know we're getting down and dirty with a twelve-bar blues in C. There was no "song", we were just riffing as we went. I'd take lead for awhile, then Joe, then Ty. Next Boxx and even David took a turn with a drum solo. Audience was right there with us, eggin' us on to get deeper down and extra dirty, and we obliged. What a great time. Ten minutes later — or was it twenty? — we were wrasslin' them twelve bars through the mud and teaching 'em who's boss. Everybody was satisfied at the end of that and I ain't lying.

No imaginary lovers for the crowd tonight, that's for sure.

"Thank you. Wow," Joe said to the crowd. "Ty. Boxx. David. And Adman. Wow." I left the stage as Joe called up the next group. "Let's get Arturo up here and give Ty a break. He deserves one. Hey, I see Ro-Ro. You want to give Boxx a rest? Come on, then. And David? Can you do a couple more? Yes? Great." Joe sure was a great Jam runner.

Folks stopped me on the way to putting up Stella with cries of *Hey, Adman. Loved it, man.* I thanked them. Drying Stella, I put her back in her case. This venue closed at eleven, so it wasn't long before Joe shut it down with all the horns who wanted to join on stage. With *shave and a haircut, two bits,* Joe thanked the audience and came down off the stage and over to my table with a glass of Gentry Bourbon. He took a sip and sat down.

"So, tell me about this performance shed thing you got going on."

"CC and I bought sixty acres in West Georgia, heading out I-20. We're boarding horses and got stands of pine for harvesting. I've got a recording studio in the house. Workshop out near the barn. Dad and I built a large performance area in a shed style. Stage. Lighting. Sound."

"How big's the stage?" Joe asked.

"Big enough to hold your Really Big Band."

He whistled. "Nice."

"My whole thing is to bring Jazz, and other music, too, to the area where smaller shows can be held affordably."

"You gonna sell food and drinks?"

"Depends. We won't do it ourselves. We may let food trucks come out for certain events, we're still working on all that, but mostly it will be BYOB & BF & CB."

"What the heck is that?"

"Bring Your Own Bottle and Basket of Food and Chairs/Blanket, too. CC thought that up."

Joe roared a laugh. "Well, that's practical and easy. How much to rent it?"

"I know I'm doing this backward, but I haven't figured that out quite yet. I do know ticket sales will be done through my website and from that we'll take our cut and pay the rest to the act."

"Could I sell my own tickets?"

I thought about it. "I don't see why not. Got to work out how that would happen."

"Got contracts yet?"

Nodded. "Got an attorney working on all that."

He nodded. "So, this Test Jam thing…"

"Ah, anybody can come. We just want all the facilities to get a workout and let's see what we're missing, what isn't working like we want, what sort of tweaks are needed. Stuff like that."

"I'll be out of town, but I'll let my students know they should go."

I smiled. "Great. Looking forward to it. I'll text you the address and info."

We bumped fists. Joe went to pay the band and I walked Sweet Stella to the car.

On the way home, I got to thinking about what exactly Jazz is. Could it be categorized? Duke Ellington defied categories, unwaveringly refusing to conform to preconceptions of what he or his music should do. Beyond category was his greatest descriptive compliment to an artist. Duke did that better than anybody.

At the same time, there is such a thing as playing in the same key as everybody else on the same song. I once heard a story about tenor saxophonist Frank Foster who was playing a street concert in Harlem from the Jazzmobile. He called for a blues in B-flat. A young tenor player began playing notes that had absolutely no relationship to the harmonic progression or the rhythmic setting the rest of the band was playing.

So Frank stopped him and asked, "What are you doing?" The young fellow said, "Playing what I feel." At which time Frank says, "Well, feel something in B-flat, m—f—."

Only, Frank said the words.

I chuckled at that vision all the way home.

One busy week continues...

The week passed fast enough. I had a few students. Misha and I rehearsed some more. Veterinarians and owners came and went to attend to horses. I had a gig late Wednesday night for which a quartet was needed. It was not a show, just background noise at a newish effort of a chi-chi martini bar in Buckhead. Twenty-somethings, practicing sitting with elegant indifference, were taking shots at tedious conversation featuring expensive learning bought and paid for by Mommy and Daddy.

I noticed this one couple, though, that didn't seem to quite fit. They were older. He looked to be around fifty and she somewhere over forty but holding her looks nicely. From his attitude he seemed to be...how can I put it? He seemed bored and unhappy that he had to sit in *this* place listening to *that* music with *this* woman. He could barely keep from looking at the pretty young thangs sitting around him. If he had to be here he surely didn't need a wife cramping his style. The negative vibes coming from him were strong.

They were married. It was clear she was attempting to expand their horizons as a couple because the marriage was in trouble. It was also clear it wasn't going to work on him.

But, interestingly enough, she was into the music. Of all the people in the room, she was the only one listening. How did I know? At gigs like this, musicians like to work in musical "jokes" to entertain their fellow bandmates. Jokes only work when the audience understands the context. Bob Hope once died on a stage in front of thirty thousand people because the "topical" joke he told would only be understood by those who lived in California at the time. When nobody laughed, he said, "You don't have gas lines here?" The audience didn't have a clue what he was talking about. He followed that with, "Looks like I'll be getting some new joke writers."

You know what they say: If you have to 'splain a joke, then it ain't funny.

So, musicians give a lot of thought to their audience and tonight Piano showed he did just that for us when he threw in a corker and the entire band burst out laughing...

...as did that woman at the exact same time.

The band and the husband all whipped their heads around to her. She was laughing and giving us two thumbs-up and nodding. Piano threw his head back in acknowledgement of her getting the joke and the rest of us nodded and smiled her way.

But the husband pounced. He looked from her to the band and back and demanded loud enough for even us to hear, "Why are you laughing?"

She pointed to Piano. "Because he told a joke."

Hubby was confused…and mad. The band kept playing and looking from one to the other.

Drummer said quietly and sadly, "Dead Couple Walking." We nodded and played for her, only her, until they left.

I hope me and CC never become that couple.

Then Thursday morning Dad came over to start on the drawers that would go under the stage. At a reclamation place he found five, already fabricated, and thought they'd work. From narrow to wide but all long and deep, two with partitions. Looked like they came from a manufacturing plant. Very well made from wood with attached metal railing systems and metal strips protecting edges. Cheap enough, but sturdy. So he bought them in the hopes they'd work.

Misha always loves a building project, so when I told him about the drawers, next thing you know he was laying around with us — and like us, painfully finding more rocks with butts, hips, and elbows — as we crawled under the stage measuring and configuring how to attach and make them secure. We were just three boys playing in the dirt, banging and measuring and having us a fine ol' time with tools. We got one drawer installed. From that we worked out all the kinks for the install of the next four that we'd get done later.

To make those drawers work, we would have to move the sound booth. Having built it as a unit, that was easy enough. Just a matter of changing the path of the final twenty-five feet of wiring. Simple as unplugging, rerouting, and plugging back in.

Dad left, but Misha stayed for the meeting of the Amateur Sleuth Society. Ty, David, and Gerry couldn't come, but Leland, André, Carl, Chip, and Arturo showed up. While we waited on pizzas to be delivered, beers were opened and we walked to The Shed. [Hey, do you see what I did there? The Van, The Farm, and now The Shed? See? Brilliant.]

"Holy cow, Adman," André said. "This is some setup."

"Hey, look," I beckoned them to follow me. "Dad's got these drawers," I pointed to them sitting on the stage, "he's gonna build in under the stage here, here, here, and here, so we've got hidden and locking equipment storage."

"Dang." That was said by everybody.

Then I pointed to the lights and fans and overhead speakers tucked under and out of the weather. "So, as you can see, this is a high-quality setup."

Leland said, "What's it gonna cost to rent?"

"I haven't got any set base numbers yet. But…" I went on to explain about BYOB etc., ticket sales, and so forth. "Of course, the Test Jam is coming up and y'all got all the info about that, right?"

All nodded. After a bit more conversation, wherein I told them stuff you already know, we headed back to the house and got there just as the pizza delivery guy was coming up the driveway. "Anybody want to pitch in for the pizza, throw some money my way."

A few bucks came, I took some money out of the jar near the door and paid the guy. We settled in around the dining room table to discuss the matter at hand.

Misha recapped what we already knew or suspected. "So, ees been coopull weeks sense seecon' death. Ve beleef wohmahn ees murrrrderer, yes?"

Everyone nodded agreement.

"Who could it be?" Chip asked. "I mean, according to what your mother said, Adman, she's got to be a sweet person, right?"

Arturo said, "How many sweet women in Jazz do we know?"

"Let's make a list!" Leland hollered. He snapped his fingers at me, fast. "Paper! Pen!"

I tossed Leland both. He clicked the pen and we started hollering: Deb! Cath! Beth! Susan! June Bug! Marielle! Lisa!

"Slow down. Can't write that fast," Leland said, hunkered over the pad. He finally looked up and said, "More?"

Susan Two! Barbara! Lia! Marla!

"Nope. Not Marla. Mean as a dang snake," Arturo said and we agreed. Leland struck her off.

Elaine! Ro-Ro! Faith! Jaimie!

Then silence. Leland said, "I can't think of anyone else."

"Are we only talking local women?"

Leland said, "I think that would be best to stay local for now, André. You know, start with the smallest group of possibles and work from there. Yeah?"

Nods all around.

Leland said, "Okay. Here's our local list. Anybody know last names, let me know…" So with the help of Facebook and Instagram added to our personal knowledge, we found last names for thirteen women.

Leland flipped a page and wrote at the top. "In order, let's see what we know about each. First is Deb York." Leland, poised for notetaking, waited as we thought.

"I like Deb. She's sweet. Puts on a heck of show," André said. "Pays the band on time."

Leland wrote. "Anything else about Deb?"

None of us could think of anything. Finally, André said, "You know…it seems to me we should be asking why these two were murdered?"

"We've tried to see what they had in common. We couldn't find anything other than Jazz."

"Well," he continued. "Then how about this. Let's ask if Barry and Mario knew any of these singers or musicians. Wouldn't that be logical?"

"I like it," I said. "Did Deb know Barry and Mario?"

"She did." That was Chip. "I know for certain because I've seen them working gigs together."

Leland wrote that on Deb's page. "Anything else about Deb? Other than gigs, did they have any other business together? Personal relationship?"

Nobody knew and we went to the next name on the list. If pizza and beer hadn't been involved, we could probably have finished the list in an hour. We paused to eat and the beer loosened our inner comedians, so the process took more like two hours. But that's okay because when we finished, including what each does and best guesses for ages, and that they are all sweet, nice women, the list looked like this:

- Deb York, singer, 40s: Knows Barry and Mario. Played gigs with them.
- Cath, short for Catherine, Dinsmore, flute, 30s: Unknown whether she knew Mario, but does know Barry who she dated for a few weeks.
- Beth Sonander, drummer, 50s: Unknown whether she knew either victim.
- Susan Smith, singer, 30s: Unknown whether she knew Barry, but did know Mario as they were in high school together.
- June Terry, music professor, retired, 70s: Knows Barry and Mario. Seen together at Jazz jams, but no other connection discovered.
- Marielle Twain, trumpet, 40s: Also dated Barry for two years. Quite the item they were. Thought they would marry; never did.
- Susan Tordan, trombone, 20s: Unknown whether she knew either victim.
- Barbara Lightfoot, singer/guitarist, 30s: Dated Barry for a year. Devastated at the breakup. Rumored to have engaged in a little bit of stalking, but nobody had actual proof.
- Lia Sorenson, professor/singer, 50s: Taught Mario in college. Was rumored

to have had a romantic interest in him that was not returned.

- Elaine Meister, Jazz Kitten Trainee, 20s: Knows Barry and Mario from around the scene.
- Roxanne Robards, bassist, 30s: Been in Atlanta three or four years. Knows Barry, gigged together, and Mario, from around the scene.
- Faith Johnson, music student, 19: Knows Barry from around the scene. Took lessons from Mario.
- Jaimie Peerman, Jazz Kitten Trainer, 50s: Knows Barry and Mario from around the scene. Rumor was Barry had affair with her many years ago.

Everyone took pictures of the list so they could study them later. We threw boxes and bottles and cans in a trash bag, and I hauled it outside to throw later into the roll-off dumpster we had rented for construction and other junk. Goodbyes said, I went back inside.

One busy week ends

The rest of Thursday, until CC came home, was devoted to odds and ends in the life of a musician-cum-entrepreneur. Paperwork, scheduling, practicing, napping. Then supper with my honey bunch sweetie pie, dishes, a little TV and snuggling on the sofa with intermittent chats about our day. Then being shaken and told to come to bed where I could snore in peace.

I needed the sleep because I had a gig Friday, too. The setlist requested by that client would include instrumental covers of Rock songs of their choice. Just keep the beat mostly dynamic and energetic but always in the background. Done. The gig was at a Lexus car dealership throwing a party for the brand's newest models.

I watched people roll up to this invitation-only event in all brands and manners of expensive cars and, surprisingly, a few beaters, then hand over keys to the complimentary valets, young people with very good knees running everywhere fast-fast. Of course, I had my business card and brochure on display for these high rollers to take. They don't call me Adman for nothing, you know.

The band consisted of drums, sax, bass, two guitars. We set up on the stage (dealership provided that) beginning around five, started playing at six. Honchos from HQ were there. All salespeople and department managers — shined up almost as nice as the vehicles — worked the lobby, pressed the flesh, passed out business cards, and talked up the new models and all the wonderful money customers would save by buying this vehicle or that. Gearheads come in all sizes and shapes, and from every socio-economic strata. So the dealer's brand-certified master mechanics were on hand to discuss with all who wanted to delve into the specifics of engine torque and stabilizing bars and such.

Further greasing the wheels of commerce were spirits, wine, and other beverages as well as tables loaded with perfectly prepared fancy comestibles alongside iced and cracked Alaskan King Crab legs next to a heated pot of clarified butter to be poured into warmed ramekins for dipping that meat. Dang, I sure did want to dive into that, but one cannot have buttery fingers and be picking crab meat from between one's teeth when one is blowing sweet.

Above the crowd, two flexible females danced to our music on long lengths of aerial silks hung from high metal frames erected in the middle of the showroom atrium. Think Cirque du Soleil does Jazz doing Rock at Le Mans. Let me tell you this: Lexus sure does know how to throw a dang party.

A female photographer circulated all night. She was very good at getting great posed group shots and happy reactions from the crowd. She knew angles and patiently waited with her finger on the shutter button to get the best random shot she could. She said she'd send photos of the band to me…no charge. That was so sweet.

The event ended at eight, so the evening was an early one…for us. We made a pretty good fee. I had already paid the band, knew all these guys, worked with them plenty of times, so I wasn't worried they'd take the money and not show up. At one point during the evening, me and Sweet Stella went walkabout in the crowd where a few customers wanted to talk about doing an event for their business, anniversary, or third wedding. I was home by ten.

Saturday came bright and early. Roxanne was due to arrive shortly. CC had promised to go with us to The Shed and stay there while Ro-Ro was around. One should never trust a man-eater and she was a man-eater. I don't care how sweet she acted or everybody thought she was. I know a man-eater when I see one. Besides, we had a female murderer in our midst and no idea who it was. I mean, it could be her for all I knew.

Roxanne showed up at the appointed time. Together, we three walked to The Shed — CC loved the name — and Roxanne was properly impressed.

"This…is…AHHH-maaaay-zin'," Ro-Ro said.

"Thank you," we replied.

"What made you want to do this? One of those 'build it and they will come' things?"

We laughed, but I nodded. "This is truly a leap of faith. We certainly hope more folks will now have access to Jazz specifically, but other types of live music and acts that will never make it to radio or that gets lost on streaming."

"That is AHHH-maaaay-zin'. I agree. There is a lot more music out there, and much of it better, than what radio or streaming spews out." Roxanne paused momentarily. "How can I help? I mean, I assume you're not making a profit yet, right?"

We nodded again.

"Is there some work I can help with?" she said.

"Oh, yeah. Absolutely."

CC put her arm around Roxanne's shoulders and said, "That is so sweet of you to offer. John, isn't that sweet?"

I nodded vigorously. "Anytime you feel like digging rocks out of this area here, under the shed where people will be sitting, just feel free. I've got short-tined rakes and shovels." I pointed to them. "Nobody has to be here for you to come do that. Just throw the rocks in a pile and I'll put them in a wheelbarrow and put them somewhere they can be useful."

"You got it, Adman. Happy to help. Hey, I might even bring some helpers. That okay?"

CC answered, "Sure, of course. But, just let us know you're coming so we don't wonder who it is."

"Totally," Roxanne said. "I can't wait to come out for the Test Jam."

We walked her back to her car, watched as she drove away, and waved when she honked goodbye. Then back inside we went.

"I do not know why you were so worried about being alone with her," CC said. "She seems so sweet and lovely."

I bent down and looked up into CC's eyes and said, "Trust me on this, woman. She's a man-eater."

"Her? I don't believe it."

"Believe it, babe. I've known her over two years now — and heard the tales."

"Are you sure all that isn't just rumor?"

I snorted and said, "Babe, I've seen her in action. Besides, she tries it on me."

CC's eyes went wide. "What? Why, that little bitch. She better keep her hands off you."

"Oh, it's a constant battle. You would think I was the last man on earth, the way she carries on over me in public."

CC slapped me on the arm. "Stop it! Now you're just messin' with me."

"Hello! Anybody home?"

"In here, Dad."

And in walked Mom and Dad. Mom and CC had some things they wanted to do and off they went. I had time to help Dad in the workshop for about three hours, then I had to get ready for another gig. Private party at a mansion on Lake Lanier. Misha and me. Two sets tonight. Food. Drink. I loaded up a few of my albums for sale, on CD and vinyl I'd had made in a short run, plus brochures and business cards. Maybe I'd sell a few tonight. Hey, ain't nobody else gonna sell 'em for me, right?

I texted Misha I was on my way and, sure enough, he was coming out the door with his gear just as I pulled up. We stowed it in the back of The

Van, I cranked up Maps on my iPhone, put in the address, and off we went.

Fire and damnation

I woke Sunday morning to a text coming through. Smelled bacon and coffee. Grabbed my phone from the nightstand. Stumbled my way to the kitchen. Fell into a chair.

"What'll you have this morning, sugah? Wanna start with coffee?"

I smiled at CCs imitation of a Waffle House server. She bent down and kissed me as she set a hot cup of caffeine on the table. No, WH servers don't kiss ya. I stirred in sweetener and creamer. Took a sip. Then focused bleary eyes on the text onscreen. Did not recognize the number. Text said —

```
   Them: Want you to know it isn't
personal.
   Me: Who is this?
   Them: It isn't personal.
   Me: What isn't personal?
   Them: You'll find out.
   Me: When?
   Them: Soon.
```

I must've grunted because CC said, "What?"

I held the phone out for her. She took it and read the thread. "Fire and damnation!" she spat out. "Are you being stalked?"

"I don't know."

"Dad-blame-it! I hope I don't have to throw a pot of coffee in somebody's face again…give me that number. I'm gonna see who it belongs to." I must've looked horror-stricken because she said, "Don't worry. I'm taking it to work and using databases we have access to."

"Okay. But don't you be calling it." I even wagged an *I'm serious about that* finger at her.

"I won't. Text it to me." I did. Then she set a full plate in front of me. "Eat."

"Dang, woman. You're sounding just like Mama." Then I quickly added with a wink, "Not that that's a bad thing, ya know?"

CC smiled, and I ate and enjoyed. Then I went to the living room where I had dropped Sweet Stella and the box from last night's Lake Lanier gig which was filled with brochures, business cards, and the CDs and vinyl that didn't sell. Yes, I sold a few, so yay for me. I pulled the cash out of my wallet and counted it. Put it in a jar on the shelf to pay for pizza delivery. I prepped for two forty-five minute online lessons this afternoon, back to back, starting at two.

CC came into my office. "Get your boots on, boy. We're walking to the stables."

We always checked a couple of times each week to make sure no owner was neglecting their duties to the animals by keeping a dirty stall and so forth. She and I held hands and took a leisurely stroll to the barn. Everything seemed to be in order inside.

Just as we walked out of the barn, a truck towing a horse trailer rolled up, a vet's van right behind it. We waved hello.

"CC! John! Hey," she said, getting out. "How are you?"

"Good. How about you?" We shook hands with Karen Grassley, an owner.

"I'm good. Wanna let you know we're gonna be gone for a week. Got a show. Vet's here to look him over and make sure he's well and fit and help get him in the trailer."

Karen had an Andalusian, or Pure Spanish horse. Highly intelligent, they learn quickly and utterly. It was her horse who was dancing along with me and Misha when "Mi Caballo Blanco" was played. He was beautiful. Muscular and strong. Powerful hindquarters. If any horse could be said to have harmony, this Andalusian could; and rhythmic and agile, too, as we saw the other day.

"Great. Hope you win," CC said.

"Hey, Karen," I said. "Got a funny story."

"Oh, yeah? What?"

"It's about Ender," I said. Ender was the horse's name. "So, I was down at The Shed —"

"The shed?"

"Yeah. I'm building a large performance venue for outdoor concerts."

"Really? Can it be rented? For parties?"

"Yes, it can. When it's ready, I'll be sending out emails with details."

"Okay."

I continued. "So, anyway, Misha and I were testing out the sound connections. He was playing keys. All the horses came running up to the fence.

So, Misha starts playing 'Mi Caballo Blanco' and I start dancing."

Now Karen is laughing because she must know what is coming.

"So, the rest of them went back to grazing quick enough, but Ender…" I started laughing just remembering. CC is starting to giggle. "Ender was dancing right along with me doing his own show routine. When Misha stopped playing and I stopped dancing, I swear he gave us the *whut the hayle?* dirty look."

By now the vet had joined us, smiling at the story, and Karen was still laughing. Finally she said, "That boy is so smart. You see why I named him Ender, don't you?"

I continued, still laughing. "I do indeed, Karen. I do indeed."

What kind of a name for a horse is Ender, you ask? Ender is a very smart human boy — heck, a genius — whose entire life of thousands of years is the pivot upon which is set a series of space- and time-travel, dystopian, sci-fi novels by Orson Scott Card wherein Ender is the hope for saving Earth and Mankind…and soon, maybe even the Universe. See, Ender has the ability to communicate with a particular Formic Hive Queen only he doesn't know it. The Hive Queen was from a planet called Shakespeare. Also known as Bugger Bitch, she was queen of the hive. Humans demonized them as Buggers because they thought they were coming to destroy Earth. Anyway, Ender Wiggin later restores her species on Lusitania, another planet. Since he had the Hive Mind, he could…hang on…I'm getting too nerdy for you, aren't I? Thought so. I'll move on.

CC and I said hello to the vet, then waved goodbye and walked back to the house. Within a couple of hours we heard them leaving.

"There goes your dancing buddy," CC said.

"Yep. I see that. Gonna do some work before those lessons, baby." I gave her a kiss and went off to the office. Did some bookkeeping. Paid a few bills. Organized a bit of marketing and so forth. Then it was lesson time for two people; one from North Carolina, the other from Michigan, both sax players.

This Internet thing is great…until it isn't. Some people will always find a way to use a good thing for evil. Lessons done, I turned the light off in the office and went to find CC. Then I heard a ding. Email coming in. I sneaked a peak. Oooo…business opportunity. A possible gig. I turned the light back on and sat in front of the computer. A little while later, one of the guests from the dealership event was booked and deposit taken for a corporate event, a retirement party for one of their partners. Now, who can play that date with me? Misha always gets first dibs, so I sent him an email with the particulars. Then I turned the light off again and went looking for CC.

She was laying on the sofa, pillow under head and remote in hand, sound asleep. The movie she'd been watching was *The Five Pennies*, filmed in 1959. I remember watching this when I was a kid and so, now knowing this was now part of my musical history and could be my life if things went sideways, I sat at CC's feet and finished the movie. It held all the tragedy and drama life-long musicians see played out before them — heck, even befalling them — every day. The reason I like this story so much is because it's based on the real life of a man, Loring "Red" Nichols, whose very DNA was musical notes, and how he met those challenges head-on with a "little help from his friends".

The story goes that Nichols (played by Danny Kaye) is a small town cornet player who moves to New York, gets work, marries a singer. They form a band. Are successful and celebrated. Then their daughter gets polio. To get her the best care, they move to Los Angeles and have to quit the music business with all its traveling and such as that.

Time passes and the daughter, now a teenager, learns of her father's past career and tells him he should start playing again. He sure does miss it, but by now he'd lost his lip. To get it back was a huge struggle. He wants to quit. Daughter won't let him. Finally he forms a comeback tour, but it is failing.

Until…until one night players from his past come in and join him and the band. The day is saved, as they say. The giants in that film were legion, with such legends as:

Barbara Bel Geddes who would later play Miss Ellie Ewing on "Dallas", the TV show that gave us the "Who shot J.R.?" craze that went around the world. Remember that? I was just a kid, but even I was saying it on the playground.

Louis Armstrong you know, of course; he played himself in the film. Did Louis ever not play himself in a film? I'd have to look that up. Might be one of those fun facts about "Satchmo" that audiences like. Three years before he died, Armstrong was also on the 1969 soundtrack for the James Bond film "On Her Majesty's Service", the only film in the franchise featuring the best Bond there ever was, Aussie George Lazenby. Hey, even Albert Broccoli agreed with me about that.

Then there was Harry Guardino. You might remember him from the Dirty Harry movies. And Bing's brother Bob Crosby, who was quite a successful singer and actor himself. Bobby Troup, too, was in it. Did you know he wrote "Route 66", a Jazz Jam favorite with musicians and singers? Then there was Jazz drummer Shelly Manne.

Kaye's cornet playing for the film soundtrack was played by Red Nichols himself.

All this info dump just to say I was totally fan-girlin' all the way through the movie. Just as it ended, I could feel CC stretching.

She frowned. "Oh, man. Did I fall asleep? I wanted to watch the movie."

"It was great. Sorry you missed it, me wittul snorin' wu-u-u-uv mooffen."

That made her smile. "What time is it?" she said through a yawn.

I looked at my phone. "Going on seven-thirty."

We had a late supper, light; ate it out on the porch. Drank some wine.

"John?"

"Yes, me pwecious swee' pea?"

"I think it's time we got a couple of big dogs… maybe three."

When she saw my shocked expression, she laughed like she was teasing.

"I thought I told you not to."

Monday evening, CC came home from work in a state. To say she was excited would be putting it mildly. She couldn't wait to tell me.

"John, guess what?"

"Whut?" I said.

"You know that number?"

I stared at her hard. "Yeeessss?" Meaning: Yes, I do, did you call it after I told you not to? And up popped my wagging finger which she pushed away with a smile.

"I looked it up. It was one of those phones with minutes and you can get plain texting, too, and no name."

"Uuuh-hhhuuuh." Meaning: You called it didn't you? She swatted the finger away again and bounced on her tippy-toes like an excited child.

"So, I thought I'd call it."

My wagging finger popped up in the air again and this time above her head where she couldn't reach it. I reared back my head like a preacher in the pulpit condemning his Saturday night partying and hungover flock on a Sunday and let fly. "I thought I told you not to call that number. It could be dangerous."

And like the Sunday morning flock, CC ignored the admonishment and said, "Sure, dangerous, but only if they could trace the number I was calling from and get a name." She looked at me, eyes wide with perfect logic. "Right?"

My finger dropped from the air and my preacher man could see the logic, so I ended the sermon with, "Okay. Right. And?"

"Okay. I went down to street level and found a payphone."

"Aren't you smart! And…wait…there are still payphones?"

"Yes, not as many, of course. Anyway, a woman answered."

"What'd you do?"

"I went all Valley Girl on her. Changed my accent…just in case. Pretended I was calling my friend. Got started on some story about couldn't make lunch because my boss was a beee-otch and I had to work through lunch and I was sooooo sorry and could she ever forgive me."

Now I'm laughing.

"She finally manages to interrupt me —"

"You mean you allowed her to interrupt you!"

The look said duh, but her mouth yelled, "Yes!"

"Sneaky!" I held up my hand for a high five.

She slapped it. "And she says 'I think you've got the wrong number.' And I say, 'What? Oooohww.

Mah. Goooo-awd. This isn't Ginny?' And she says 'Uhhhh...nooooo.' Real snarky like. Don't like her."

"Did you recognize the voice?"

"No...well...it sounded familiar but I couldn't put a name to it. So I apologized over and over and she hung up while I was still apologizing." At that CC grinned like a cat getting ready to open a canary's cage. "Am I good or am I good?"

"You are good!" I thought for a moment and said, "Now we know it's a woman for sure." Of course, that didn't solve the problem, but it did confirm the path the Amateur Sleuth Society was on. "Guess we better be careful, huh?"

Then CC said, "I wonder if this is the same woman killing your friends?"

Of course I had already thought of that, but not mentioned it to her what with not wanting to give her bigger worries. But the cat was out of the bag now. "Yeah, I wondered about that myself, babe."

"Sounds like you should let the guys know."

"Good idea." So I went to my office and formulated an email recapping the text received, CC's hunting down the sender, and what we thought it might be. It was sent to all members of the Amateur Sleuth Society followed by a text to each:

```
Check your email.
```

The rest of Monday evening was filled with replies. Most of which were that it was obvious we needed to meet again. Somebody suggested Thursday and that seemed okay with everybody. I proposed everybody bring some sort of food and beer as my fridge was not stocked. Got lots of thumbs-up in reply. I put it on my calendar.

Tuesday morning I got another text from that same no-name number. It said

```
Her: remember not personal
Me: WHAT ISN'T PERSONAL?
Her: u soon find out
Me: HOW SOON?
```

There was no more reply. So I thought, you know, she has my number. Why don't I just call her myself. Obviously, she knows me. If she knows me and is using an anonymous phone — I think they're called burners, I'd have to ask Detective Love about that — it is again quite obvious I could probably recognize her voice. What did I have to lose? I called the number.

It rang and no voice mail came on and nobody answered. That elicited a text.

```
Her: yeah I'm not stupid
Me: ONE CAN ALWAYS HOPE.
Her: ur funny
Me: HOW MANY YOU GONNA KILL?
Her: ain't u just a smart boy
```

Calling Detective Love

Ah-ha! Now it is confirmed: We know each other. One more clue to tell the guys so we can drill down further. Oh, yes. I do believe this anonymous texter is the murderer.

What could I do about it? There ain't enough to take to the police. I mean, really. What am I gonna say? "I got this text and I don't know who it is but…?" Besides, which jurisdiction would I call? Hey, wait. Hang on. I know who to call. Did I still have her business card? I went to my office and looked in the drawer where I always put business cards. It was a mighty impressive collection. I began gently digging through the pile. Whew, I found it.

"Detective Love," she answered.

"Hello, Detective Love. You may not remember me. I'm John Dann. My wife and I…you know… restrained that serial killer kidnapper dude a few years back that was killing the —"

"I remember. Jazz people. How can I help you?"

"You may not have heard, but there's been two suicides of friends of mine."

"So, if they are suicides, why you callin' homicide?"

"Good question. Give me a minute to explain."

I paused and waited. Then Detective Love said, "Okay. Shoot."

"These two friends died by poisoning themselves. Not only that. They are in the Jazz community and —"

"Were they having an affair?"

"I don't think so." Then more quickly, "But there's more. Hang on."

Love waited, then I continued. "It is my opinion that a woman managed to poison both of these victims. The reason I'm saying is that I got several texts, one of which said *just remember, it isn't personal.* My wife…you remember CC?"

Love gave an enthusiastic yes, and said, "What's the brand of your new coffeepot?"

"Cuisinart."

"That's a good one." Then she waited.

Hey, I'm good with cues. I saw mine and continued. "Okay, so CC went to a payphone and called the number to see who answered. It was a woman. Then a couple of days later I get more texts with the same messaging. So I thought why don't I call it. So I did. Here's what happened…"

```
Her: yeah I'm not stupid
Me: ONE CAN ALWAYS HOPE.
Her: ur funny
Me: HOW MANY YOU GONNA KILL?
Her: ain't u just a smart boy
```

I shut up and waited. I heard a tapping sound, then, "Hmmm...what's the number?" I gave it to her. I did not tell her CC had already looked it up since, you know, that might be illegal or something. Then she said, "I'll get back to you," and hung up.

Fifteen minutes later, she called back. "Mr. Dann? It's a burner."

"Does that mean it can't be traced?"

"Kinda sorta. What are your friends' names?"

"Barry Lamon and Mario Alberto Mireles."

"Where did they die?"

"I don't know."

I heard a sigh. "Georgia? Metro Atlanta?"

"I really don't know. I know where they lived."

I heard another sigh. "Where did they live?" I gave her that information. "Okay. I'll look into it and let you know." Then she hung up.

Alrighty. We're rolling. I'll just let the police handle it. Was this just wishful thinking? What if the murderer was coming for me? How would she get poison into me without a fight or me even knowing? Holy crap. What if she was coming for CC? Now I was freaking out and I stayed freaked out until CC got home.

"CC. My love. My dearest. My wittul wuv mooffin honey bunch o' wuv. Ummmm..."

She screwed up her face and said, "What?"

"Baayyybeee. Huuuney. I called the number."

"And..."

"And she didn't answer."

"Then..."

"Then she sent me a text." I pulled out my phone and gave it to her. She read the text thread.

"So…"

"So…then I called Detective Love and told her everything. She's going to look into it."

"Okay." She walked into the kitchen.

I followed so close I was almost tripping on her heels. "But, baby. Huuuuney. See, I'm worried. What if this person knows us well enough that we don't suspect them? And what if they get close enough to me…[I gulped]…or you, and manages to get one or both of us to ingest poison?"

She stopped making a pot of coffee, turned to me, and shrugged. "Easy. We don't eat or drink anything that a female — except your mother — tries to give us. We do not eat or drink anything we don't know from whence it came."

She turned her attention back to the pot and left me standing there with my mouth hung open. "That was easy, makes sense. So, okay. Handled then?"

"Handled." She hit the start button. "You know I work for attorneys, right?"

"When was the last time I told you I loved you?"

She thought for a moment and said, "If memory serves, I believe it was last night."

"That was when I showed you I loved you."

She patted my cheek and said, "Actions do speak louder than words, you hunk-o' hunk-o' burnin' luurrrv."

"Sounds like a song idea. But I might just need some more inspiration to write it."

"Well —"

She was interrupted by the phone ringing. It was Leland. I answered.

"Adman, you're never gonna guess."

I could tell from his voice this was not good news. "What happened?"

"I just heard that Angela Peterson committed suicide…poison."

"What the heck? Who'd you hear it from?"

"Boxx called me. Said he heard it from Ragtime."

I knew Ragtime, he was a good slider; we'd played together in Joe's Big Band. "I'll call him. Thanks, Leland."

"Another one?" CC asked as I hung up and began scrolling through my contact list. I nodded, saw Ragtime's name, and called him.

"Adman! Long time, man," Ragtime answered.

"Hey, how you doing?"

"Oh, just keepin' on keepin' on. One foot in front of the other."

"Great. Hey, Leland just called me and told me about Angela Peterson's suicide. How'd you hear about it?"

"Man, that's so sad. Let me think. How did I hear about it?" He paused and thought. "I 'member. I overheard it at Kat's."

"When did she die?"

Ragtime sighed. "I do not know."

"Okay. I'll go on her Facebook page and see if her family is…oh, hang on. I'll call Michael at Red Light Café."

"Yeah. He might know. Didn't she have some sort of monthly event out there?"

"Yeah-yeah-yeah. She has a songwriters' club on Meetup. They been meeting at RLC for, geez, maybe six years or so, I think."

"Let me know what you find out, Adman. Okay?"

"I will. Later."

Michael was the next to get a text:

```
You hear about Angela Peterson's
suicide?
```

My phone rang. I answered. "Yo, Michael. Whaddaya know?"

"Yes, I heard about it. She did not kill herself. She had three shows booked in the next six months. We were talking details and marketing the night before she supposedly killed herself. Plus her club meetings. I'm telling you, she did not kill herself."

"I agree. When did she die?"

"This was…ummm…three days ago."

"And you heard how she died?"

"Poison is what I heard. Listen to me, Adman. There is no way in the world Angela killed herself. It did not happen. She had to have been murdered."

"You know Barry Lamon and Mario Mireles, right?"

"I went to Barry's funeral, but I didn't know Mario."

"Both of them also died from poison."

"I did not know that."

"Where was Angela found?"

"I think at home."

"So were the other two…at least that's what I heard. Do you know where she lived?"

Michael hollered to his wife. "Hey, Ellen. Do you know where Angela Peterson lived?"

I heard her holler back at him from another room but couldn't make it out. He came back on. "Ellen says she lived in Decatur, just ITP."

"Okay. Thanks. Talk to you later."

I disconnected the call and looked at CC. "I'm going to call Detective Love in the morning and tell her the latest."

CC nodded. "That's a good idea. You should also text the guys and tell them."

I did, by which time the coffee was ready and we had a cup and a slice of cake Mom had brought over the other day. Then it was Goodnight, Irene, and we fell into bed where the sandman kissed us both good and hard and we were gone.

Calling Detective Love...again

I called Detective Love first thing Wednesday morning and gave her all the details of the latest victim, Angela Peterson.

"Detective Love, I'm wondering how it is the killer can get poison into these people in the privacy of their own homes."

"Could be gifts...sent through the mail... hand delivered...sent by UPS...food, liquid. But I have to find out what kind of poison and if it was the same for all victims."

"Ah. Okay. All I've heard are rumors about Barry Lamon...something about eating poison in cookies, but he didn't seem like much of a baker."

"Didn't cook?"

"Nah. He acted like he was a playa. Oh, he liked the ladies. And ate out all the time."

"Okay. Thanks. I'll check it out," she said. Then, "He have a wife or girlfriends that cooked for him?"

"Divorced a long time. Girlfriends? Plenty, to hear him talk. Ummm...I'm sure some of them cooked. He could put on a fine pitiful act when he wanted to."

Love chuckled and said, "You saying he can bring out the mother in the ladies?"

"I am saying that, yes."

Love hooted a laugh, said goodbye, and hung up. As CC had explained to me once upon a time: Bad guys like to hang around cases and make themselves useful to the popo to find out what they knew. So, I was under no illusions that Detective Love would share any information with me. After all, I had not forgotten a few years ago when I said something about the Amateur Sleuth Society and her partner, Detective Mick Hepcutts, had said, "Hey, your society's acronym is A.S.S." Then they had laughed… snickered actually. It was funny. My feelings were not hurt.

All of that reminded me of what had recently happened with the World Taekwondo Federation. For years their acronym had been — with no problems — WTF. Until, that is, somebody pointed out to them that WTF was now shorthand around the world in texts, tweets, posts, and wherever adults were sparing assaults on little kids' ears but who still wanted to share their shock using the F-bomb and a question mark. So shorten their acronym to WT the Federation did, and changed their logo, got new banners, and updated website and business cards.

The Amateur Sleuth Society is different. We're gonna stick to our guns and remain A.S.S. members because it was these A.S.S. members who helped break that other case wide open and catch a serial killer. I think if you delved into her heart of hearts, Detective Love knew and appreciated that and couldn't wait for us to call with more clues.

And so to help with more clues, I sent a text to the group:

```
Third "SUICIDE". Poison. Angela
Peterson. Summit? Thurs? Same time? Same
bat channel?
```

All whose schedules were free said they would bring beer and pizza. See how we A.S.S. members support each other in the fight against crime, I mean, in the quest to find our friends' killer? We've got each other's backs, that's for sure, and that is not in any way, shape, or form a pun.

I went out to The Shed with my to-do and to-get lists to see what else needed to be added. Also, wanted to determine where best to put directional signage. You know, park here, sit here. Then I got to thinking. Holy cow. What about bathrooms? Dang. Was I going to have to hire portable units or was I going to have to build a unisex bathroom? Time to call Dad.

"What's up, John?"

"That's what I'm calling about, Dad. Wanna know what we forgot?"

"Sure."

"Toilets."

Silence. Then a whispered *crap!*

"Exactly. I don't think we want to be building any facilities. Maybe we should look into leasing portable toilets? And we would need one wheelchair accessible, too. Right?"

"That sounds like a plan. Want me to look into it? I got a friend who rents and services them."

"That would be great. Thanks. Remember, this Saturday for the Test Jam."

"What time?"

"Seven-thirty p.m."

And so after a little chit-chat, I hung up just as CC got home from work. Like a good husband should, I met her at the door with a big hug and a "Whut's fer supper, you bewitchin' babe you?"

Like a good wife fresh from her job, she hugged me in return, gave me a little spank, and replied, "I don't know. Whut'd ya cook?"

Ahhhh...I bet you're thinking "She gotcha good there, Adman!" But you would be wrong. And let me tell you why. It's because you were not informed of everything I did today. I only told you the interesting parts. In fact, I had washed, dried, folded, and put up two loads of laundry. I'd made my famous secret-seasoning hamburger patties and thick-sliced sweet onions, and local-grown tomatoes, skint of course. For you Ro-Ro's out there: Skint in this instance means peeled. Put it all in the fridge ready to surprise my honey bunny. And when I was on the phone with Dad, I was firing up the grill. And not a gas grill, either. Real charcoal with some Jack Daniel's woodchips for flavor, thank you very much. I proceeded to tell my honey bunny just that.

"Baby, the charcoal is just about ready," I said. Then with a wink, "Oooo-yeah, got da fire burnin' hot for ya, woman."

She stared hard with no smile. "ETA my plate?"

"Thirty minutes?"

She stared again, nodded. "Alrighty then. I'mma gonna go change. Be back shortly. What's yer drink order, big boy?"

"Duh. What I always drink with burgers."

"Beer it is." With that she whipped around and headed to the bedroom.

In the meantime, I was pulling out all the fixin's and plates and a big platter to put the finished patties on. I always cooked extra and put them back in the freezer for easy eating later, so, yeah, I would need a big platter. Wasn't long and there I was sweating over hot coals when a cold one was slid into my free hand. I put the bottle against my forehead. Sure felt good. CC silently went back inside where I knew she would be slicing Ciabatta rolls and grilling them in butter.

"Hey, babe?" I hollered.

"Yes, John?" she hollered back.

"Five minutes until I pull them off the grill."

"Yay!"

Yay was right. It was delicious. Before long, supper was over, dishes done. I kissed CC goodbye, but that wasn't a problem because we'd both had thick slabs of fresh onion on our burgers so we canceled each other out. Then me and Sweet Stella was a-heading out to RLC where we arrived by nine-thirty.

"Adman! Whutcha been up to, man?"

"Hey, Mitchie." He tried to wave me through, but I handed over the door fee anyway since I'd gotten there so early. Normally, I'm arriving later and he lets me slide on in without paying. But he didn't turn it down. "Been busy as heck. How 'boutchew?"

"Cain'tchew tell? Livin' the dream." We laughed and I went on through the doors.

I waited until the door closed before I walked in further. Blowing sweet on the stage to my left was Skywalker, eyes closed, so he didn't see me come in. Michael saw me all the way from the back at the bar and raised his eyebrows in *Your usual?* I nodded and gave a two thumbs-up and headed back to the bar. Young lions were out in force tonight, so walking to the bar was a carefully orchestrated event. Instrument cases were everywhere. I kicked a few that were blocking the dark aisle and gave the young owners a look that said *Bad manners, dude.* They quickly stowed their cases properly. Those did not get a fist bump from The Adman and I could only hope they learned the lesson.

You can't put people — fans, especially! — in danger of falling. Where were these boys raised? In a barn? Geez! I was sounding just like my daddy. Anyway, after fist-bumping to "Hey, Adman" from a bunch of folks and making nice with fans I recognized as regulars at the jam, I finally made it back to the bar. I took Stella off my back and tucked her between a stool and the bar, all nice and cozy…and out of the way of feet.

"Start a tab tonight, Adman?" Michael asked.

"Yeah, let's do that. How you doing, Michael?"

"Good. Not as busy tonight with paying customers, though."

"Yeah, I see all the broke students." I took a sip and let it warm my throat. "Ellen here tonight?"

"Yeah. She's back in the kitchen. Seems cheese and fruit plates are quite popular this late eve. Want some?"

"Nah. Just finished supper before I got here. Thanks, though."

I turned to the stage, now crowded with four more horns, and perused the crowd. They looked like they were thoroughly enjoying the competition between the young ones. When Skywalker got cheeky with his horn and blew witty, real fans laughed, but the youngsters just look confused. Give them time, I thought, just give them time.

Then one of the youngsters decided he would try to be as witty, but he didn't understand the underlying joke that made it funny in the first place, therefore he did not get the same audience reaction. I watched as he became more confused and blew it all again, harder, faster, more complicated, quickly turning off the audience. Skywalker let him have his moment, then stepped in and took over to bring the thing back on track. They finished with a bang and a hard stop and the audience clapped loudly.

Skywalker stepped to the mic and said, "What do you think about these Young Lions, tonight? Think they have a future?" More applause as the youngsters stood there like deer caught in a headlight. "Alright. Let's let Monroe have a break on the drums. We've got a young drummer here tonight with his dad. Wanna come up and play? Yeah? Alright. He's only ten years old."

More applause as the boy timidly climbed the steps. He sat, adjusted the throne, and pulled out his sticks. Dad was beaming from the audience, smartphone in hand, recording the event for Mother to see when they got home.

"Let's get Mark up here on keys. We got any other bass players here tonight?" He put a hand above his eyes to shield the stage lights so he could see out into the audience. "I see you, Emma. Come on up. And who do I see back at the bar? How'd you sneak in past me, Adman? I'll get you up in a few."

I waved to him and any in the audience who turned around to get a look at the world famous me.

"Soooo…where are our vocalists tonight? Anybody?" No vocalists spoke up, so Skywalker talked with the band to see what they wanted to play. Somebody chose "Days of Wine and Roses" in D. Skywalker got them started just as Ruby Grace came in. He stepped down from the stage and whispered in her ear. She nodded in the affirmative and stood next to the stage.

Skywalker let the band play for a bit, then went back up and said something. They all kept playing, nodded, and Ruby Grace went on the stage. The band quieted down and Mark hit a solid D on the keyboard and held it while Ruby began, *rubato* — that is, free and easy with time, only the horn echoing her at first.

> The…days… [horn]
> of wine and ro-o-oses…[horn]
> [horn] *[She looked at the lights]*…
> laugh and run away…[horn]
> like a child…at pla-a-a-ay…[horn].
> [horn] *[She looked at the audience]*…
> Through a meadowland

toward a closing do-o-o-or…
[horn] a door marked 'never more'…
that wasn't there…before."

She looked at Mark and nodded. Then drums, bass, and keys joined her as they all ramped up to a slow and even tempo to finish out the tune.

Ah, the audience sure did love it when Ruby Grace sang. Hers was not a typical Jazz voice and she didn't try to be a typical Jazz singer. She wasn't professionally trained and didn't want to be The Star. She was a songwriter who, to get her songs heard, was forced to overcome her aversion to the stage and sing. Ruby was not averse to The Great American Songbook. She only liked certain standards and only as long as she could sing them her way…which, as we all remember, is a great American state of mind. Singing was not a first love because with her the writing always comes first. Always and forever: Words first, then music.

I know Skywalker said he'd call me up in a bit, but it was Ruby Grace singing and I heard Stella hollering at me from her case, so she and I skedaddled up to the stage and joined in with Skywalker, Mark, the little red-headed kid on drums, and Emma. The kid didn't know who I was, but the daddy certainly did. He was quite excited to get footage of his son playing drums behind me.

Three hours later, jam over, chats had, I settled my tab and headed home.

An email notification came in. The photos from the Lexus dealership event had arrived. Wow. They looked good, too.

A.S.S. Summit

Thursday dawned bright and early for CC. She was such a happy morning person. For me it simply dawned with Dad hollering from the kitchen.

"Who wants an Egg McMuffin, hashbrowns, and coffee?"

Dad did not have to call twice. What a perfect breakfast. Toasted, buttered English Muffin. Egg cooked in a little ring. Cheese. Slice of Canadian Bacon...or these days, a patty of sausage if you prefer. Deep-fried hash brown patty salted with that superfine salt they use. And yes, I like Mickey D's coffee, too. Even highbrow food snobs covertly indulge. I know this for a fact because plenty of publicly avowed vegans who shake fingers in the faces of carnivores do the walk of shame when the craving hits them for this perfect breakfast combo.

"Thanks, Dad. Cream is in the fridge."

"No need. They fixed our coffees already."

"Whoo-hoo, Mickey D's," I said and we dug in.

Didn't take us long to finish this particular nectar of the gods, then out we went to work some more on the drawer installations under the stage. Laying in the cool dirt working on a project with Dad, listening to the wind through the trees, hearing the distant echo of horses gamboling, doing what I love, sleeping with a high-quality woman, well I'll tell you, life doesn't get any better.

Two more drawers done and it was time for the Amateur Sleuth Society to start showing up. I took a broom to Dad to knock off all the dirt from his back before he got in his car to go home; then I went inside to shower. I had texted the guys to let them know the door was unlocked and to come on in. Misha and Chip had arrived by the time I shut off the shower. I quickly dried and threw on shorts and T-shirt. A pizza box was open. Grabbing a slice of Papa John's, I dipped it in that garlic butter they send and slurped a big bite. Breakfast had long since worn off and this sure did taste good. Thirsty, I twisted the top off a beer and it was bottom's up.

"Eeess nize to sleep late, Jaaahhnnn."

"Is it? These days I don't know what that's like anymore." Misha looked amused. Chip was confused, so I explained. "Dad got here early. We were out there working on the storage drawers."

"Heyyy! Why you no call me?" Misha did love a good project.

I chuckled. "Truth be told, I did not expect him this morning and was looking forward to a good lie-in. We got two more drawers installed and —"

"Pizza Hut is delivered!" Ty hollered from the front door.

"In the kitchen," I yelled.

Ty walked in with two large and slid them on top of the table. "Misha. Chip. Adman." Fist bumps all around. "Where's the beer?"

Chip passed a bottle to Ty and I continued. "More than likely he'll be back tomorrow morning to get the other two finished. Want me to confirm that with Dad and let you know?"

Misha nodded and sucked on the cold bottle of beer. I texted Dad with the question while the guys talked. Within fifteen minutes Carl, Arturo, André, and Leland arrived bearing food and beer. The phone rang. It was Dad.

"Hey, Dad…I can work tomorrow…Yeah… Right…Misha wants to come…Yeah…Hang on …Misha! Dad says he's gonna be out here at eight…"

Misha gave a thumbs-up. "I be here."

"Dad?...Yeah, Misha says he'll see you in the morning…Okay…Love ya." I turned to the group. "Okay. Have y'all been studying that list of nice women we know?"

Arturo spoke up. "I have. Here's what I've been thinking. I marked off my list any woman I've known well and a long time. Ones I just cannot imagine would turn to serial or spree murder."

That created a huge agreement among the guys upon which we decided to review each one. So, we pulled out our list of females and asked ourselves: Who did we not know enough about? Who was new to our circle? I went to the computer and printed out a copy of the list. By way of review, on it were:

- Deb York, singer, 40s: Knows Barry Lamon and Mario Mireles. Played gigs with them.
- Cath, short for Catherine, Dinsmore, flutist, 30s: Unknown whether she knew Mario Mireles, but does know Barry who she dated for a few weeks.
- Beth Sonander, drummer, 50s: Unknown whether she knew either victim.
- Susan Smith, singer, 30s: Unknown whether she knew Barry, but did know Mario as she hired him for a gig.
- June Terry, music professor, retired, 70s: Knows Barry and Mario. Seen together at Jazz jams, but no other connection discovered.
- Marielle Twain, trumpet, 40s: Also dated Barry for two years. Quite the item they were. Thought they would marry; never did.
- Susan Tordan, trombone, 20s: Unknown whether she knew either victim.
- Barbara Lightfoot, singer/guitarist, 30s: Dated Barry for a year. Devastated at the breakup. Rumored to have engaged in a little bit of stalking, but nobody had actual proof.
- Lia Sorenson, professor/singer, 50s: Taught Mario in college. Was rumored to have had a romantic interest in her that was not returned.

- Elaine Meister, Jazz Kitten Trainee, 20s:
  Knows Barry and Mario from around
  the scene.
- Roxanne Robards, bassist, 30s: Been in
  Atlanta three or four years. Knows
  Barry, gigged together, and Mario from
  around the scene.
- Faith Johnson, music student, 19: Knows
  Barry from around the scene. Took
  lessons from Mario.
- Jaimie Peerman, Jazz Kitten Trainer, 50s:
  Knows Barry and Mario from around
  the scene. Rumor was Barry had affair
  with her many years ago.

Leland said, "Let's do it like this. Adman, call
out a name. Then I'll ask who's known her for less
than…what?"

André said, "Less than five years?"

"Okay. That should start narrowing down the
list, right? Okay, Adman. Name."

"Deb York," I called.

Leland said, "Less than five. Hands." Only Chip
knew Deb less than five years. "Agreed? She's off
the list?"

Nods all around. We went through the rest of
the list like that and were left with five names:

- Cath Dinsmore
- Susan Smith
- Elaine Meister
- Roxanne Robards
- Faith Johnson

"Now," Carl said, "of those who would most likely be such a killer?"

"Elaine Meister. No way," Misha said.

"Why do you say that, Misha?" Arturo asked.

"Elaine eees not eeeevul."

"I agree with Misha," André piped in. "She is very pretty and very sweet and definitely is a total fan. I've never seen her be mean. I've never seen her be anything but supportive. She would totally have to be insane to do this and I don't think she is."

"Strike her name off the list?" Leland looked at the show of hands. "Strike her off."

I complied and called out the next name. "Susan Smith."

Leland counted. "So we keep her on?"

"Ummm…"

"Ummmm what, Chip?"

"Ummmm…I've known her pretty good… just…not long."

"What does that mean?" Carl asked.

"How long have you known her?" Leland said. "You know. How long?"

"Well, Leland, a couple of years. And Carl, it means that we had a…uhh…a…ummm…"

Misha piped up. "Roockin' zee van?"

It took the rest of us a couple of beats to get his meaning, then we all turned to Chip and smiled. He blushed. I kid you not, he blushed hard.

"We never did it in a van!" he said indignantly.

"Zen, my frin, you have meeesed out on loats of foon," Misha teased.

We couldn't help but laugh.

"So," said Arturo. "You telling us we have to strike her off the list because you shared a sausage with her?"

Chip said heatedly, "No! I think we should see if she fits other parameters...before... before we knock her off."

"You mean before we decide to strike her off the list?" Arturo clarified. "Not kill her, knock her off?"

Chip just rolled his eyes. I said, "Chip, you act like you're still in love with her." And he blushed some more.

Leland, master of the ceremony, said, "Agreed. Other parameters. What else do we know about Susan? Is she a professional singer or one who just does it for a hobby?"

"Hobby. I've never seen or heard of her doing a paying gig. She never has any shows. Where does she work?"

Chip said, "She sells real estate."

The vote was to strike Susan off the list. We also struck off Cath Dinsmore. That left Roxanne Robards and Faith Johnson. Both were new to the Atlanta Jazz scene. Roxanne had been around two to three years and Faith, a student at GSU in the Jazz Studies program, had been here about eight months.

"Alrighty," Leland said. "We're down to two. Now what do we do?"

Everybody turned to me. "I think I should call Detective Love and tell her what we think." They all nodded and thus the meeting ended. That is, it almost ended.

"Hey, guys. *YA koye-chto pomnyu!* Ummm...I remember sumpsing!"

"Whaddya 'member?" That was Chip speaking for all of us.

"About Rohcksahn Rohbardhs," he said. "She mad at me. We write song togezzer, but she seenks I...errrr...stole it."

"Huh?" That was all the rest of the guys.

"I remember that. It's been about a year or so ago. And...?" I looked at Misha.

"Nussing. Just *chto-to*....remember."

"Fighting over royalties. Another good reason not to cross her off the list." We all laughed hard at that joke and the meeting was now truly over.

Misha and Adman play a gig

Misha stayed for awhile after the guys left Thursday afternoon. I had a baby grand at the house, so he played that and we got some rehearsal time in for our upcoming tour. Rehearsal time is for refining the presentation, not writing new material. That means we critique each other and go over the same bits multiple times until we're finally happy with it. Plus, we make notes on charts to remind ourselves of what we finally settled on.

Contrary to what a lot of people think, musicians each have their own interpretation of a piece. So, while the audience may hear — oh, let's say "Caravan" — a standard they are familiar with because the bones and theme of the song are intact, what differentiates one version from another is how the musician plays it in any given performance. In Jazz that is expected by the listener and it does not throw them for a loop. Whereas in Rock and

Country, you don't mess with standards. The closer to the original you get, the happier the audience is.

Neither is right or wrong to the exclusion of the other. That's just the reality. My opinion on this — and I've made a study of it — is that in live shows featuring Rock and Country, the audience sings along. They especially love their hooks. To go off on a tangent is to mess with that fun. It's bad manners. Unless you train the audience to expect tangents, and that's kind of not the norm in those genres. So in those two particularly, if tangents are indulged in by the band, they are planned out well ahead of time and the audience is given multiple audible or visual clues of what's coming and they settle in for a fun side trip and the band will always lead them right back to what is familiar and that's what they end with and everybody goes home happy.

But in Jazz. Wow. That's a special case. Tangents can come anywhere at anytime and the audience will love it as long as they can tell it's a tangent. This is a particular pet peeve of mine. You see, sometimes we Jazz musicians will take a tangent that is so understated only other musicians will be able to recognize it. That's why you sometimes see Jazz musicians on a stage laughing like they're sharing a joke and you wonder what you missed. What you missed was the inside joke because the audience's ear is not that finally tuned. All they heard was the bones of the standard.

I can hear you ask, "Adman, aren't you being just a little bit persnickety and snobbish about this matter?" To that I say No! and here's why: It's all about the money. Let me explain.

I have bills to pay. Who doesn't? Working musicians don't get a weekly paycheck we can depend on. We get paid through ticket sales at venues for our own shows. We get hired as sidemen (where we back up a featured performer but we ourselves are not the main draw). We're hired to play for private functions (usually pretty good money) or in a hotel lobby or banquet room as pleasant background noise (usually easy gigs). We teach. Those of us who are headliners sell our own recordings, T-shirts, etc., also known as merch.

In other words, multiple streams of income. It's not a secret most of us would starve if we had to rely solely on one category of income. One kind of revenue that has seen declining numbers in recent years is sales of recordings. I have an opinion on why that is — one that is shared by others, by the way. Here it is:

Too many Jazz musicians forget the needs and limitations of the buying public.

What that means is this. Let's say the musician is covering the standard "Come Fly With Me", a famous song by Frank Sinatra. The musician has studied the song inside and out, so when he makes a change to it he believes is witty, other musicians hear it; to them it is a different version. But to the audience, it's just a regular "Come Fly With Me". Now, let's say that hundreds of Jazz musicians record that song and hope to sell it, but their changes are only what other musicians can hear. After a while, when the buying audience sees "Come Fly With Me" on an album next to many other famous standards, they say, "I already have that." Naturally, they don't buy the album and sales decrease.

We've done a good job of training the audience by forgetting to overtly surprise them. Some have said we've gotten lazy. Others have said we've focused too tightly on the myth of what Jazz is all about. Still others have said we've become afraid to truly experiment. Fear of audience reaction — or of bucking the prevailing wisdom of self-appointed experts whose good opinion we seek — also keeps us in a deadly downward descent into not being able to support ourselves.

I'm not picking on Jazz here; this state of affairs is not unique to it. Think of any musical genre or any type of performing art, books, and so forth. Each has stagnated at various times with the public; each must be shaken up. Sometimes that shake-up gives us Disco (Lord, help us), but guess what? There were some solid, excellent songs that came out of that experiment and gave ideas to others who then took it further.

Whew! There I go again…preaching. I am so sorry...but not sorry, too.

Anyway, after Misha left, I called Detective Love to fill her in on what A.S.S. had come up with and how. She thanked me and said she'd be in touch.

Then I set about giving Sweet Stella a thorough cleaning. Misha and I had a gig Friday night, tomorrow, at the retirement party for a partner in a law firm, and I wanted Stella to shine for the big spenders. I hired Big Lou on drums, Deb York on vocals, and Boxx on bass. We weren't going to get fancy on them. A solid set of standards from the youth of the retiring partner pretty much made up our setlist. Yeah, his wife and kids put the list together. All these songs meant something to the family. Probably interwoven with life events and, since a retirement party is another time to look back at a full life, thus apropos.

So on Friday night it was appropriate to be as overt as possible with keeping strictly to the bones of the songs, our creative artistry be damned, our *artistes* kept in check.

It was their night. It was their story. We would be there for them.

And we were. I suggested the partner and his wife lead a dance. With the opening notes of a song, the partner had tears in his eyes and his wife was looking at him with all the love in the world. I surprised them with one Paul Anka made famous called "Times of Your Life". Written by songwriters Bill Lane (lyrics) and Roger Nichols (melody), it was first recorded as a jingle for Kodak's US advertising campaign. Paul, thirty-four, next recorded it for a Canadian release of his 1975 album after which it became a big hit single in the United States, too. The lyrics are phenomenal.

And by the end of the song, with Deb emoting so beautifully on the lyrics, the entire audience was crying and smiling and laughing and clapping in honor of this man's legacy.

We creatives serve The Muse, but Music must always serve the needs of the listener.

Harold moves in

Today, Saturday, was the day for the Test Jam. It would start around seven-thirty this evening, so I needed my rest and slept in. CC said she'd see me later and something about Mom and Dad, then a goodbye kiss I barely remembered because I was sleeping hard. Didn't even hear the door shut. Waking midmorning, I puttered about, finally settled in front of the TV, coffee in one hand, a Dunkin' in the other. Yawning between bites and not even paying any attention to the time.

However, CC had not forgotten about her need for a dog…or three. She'd told Mom and Dad about it and that she wanted them to be big dogs, not yappy lap dogs. Dogs that could run the property and fight off a bad guy by tearing out his throat, not biting his ankle like a pesky chigger. They said the best way to go was to get a rescue mutt.

Should be easier looking after dogs than kids, and since we weren't going to be having any kids,

who was I to complain? *Whoozagootboy? Izagootboy!*
Yes, indeed. Still, they need their vaccines and their
food and water, so we had to figure out how to
house and care for them.

The dogs could not come in the recording
studio. Allergies stopping up throats and nasal
cavities of people wanting to sing was not a good
thing to greet you upon renting recording space. So
we'd have to close that off from whatever pack we
ended up with. Of course, all that was hypothetical
conversations we'd had for a possible future. No
details settled. Like talking about what color to paint
the new baby's nursery while the wife is still on The
Pill and the husband's bedside drawer was stocked
with condoms.

It was cute but nothing was gonna change.

Then ding went my text. It was CC.

`Almost home. Surprise. Outside in five.`

Stuffing the rest of a second doughnut in my
mouth, off went the TV, and out I went. Mom and
Dad drove up first. They got out of the car, smiling
and excited.

"John, wait and see!" Mom said, clapping hands
like a little girl with a new dolly.

CC parked the car and that's when I saw a dog
sitting in the back, looking out the window. She got
out and opened the car door I was now standing in
front of. "Come on, Harold. Come on, boy."

"Harold?"

"Don't make fun of his name or he won't get
out." Harold jumped out of the car, trotted over to
CC and stood by her. They were both looking at me.

"I won't. Just wondering that's all." What the heck kind of name was Harold?

CC was fast telling me his story. "After fifty years of marriage there was this old woman. Lost her husband. Harold. So to keep from being lonely, a friend gave her a puppy. She loved him. But she died and her family had no way of taking the dog. He's four. See?" CC's arm swept three-sixty on our horizon. "Harold can live out the rest of his life where a dog can have some fun rootin' around, chasin' squirrels, and playing with horses."

"Baaaaabeeee. I was not aware we were getting a dog."

CC's face fell. "But...we talked about it."

"Yes, we *talked*. I just wasn't expecting it so soon. And he's so big."

Her chin quivered. "But...but..." Then she looked from Harold to me. I looked at Harold. Yeah, he'd seen his cue and took it. With head and belly hung low and haunches all peaked up, sad eyes rolled my way.

Harold was a big mixed breed. One of those Heinz 57 types. A little bit of this, that, and the other, and boom, with the best of them all a great dog is born. One of those dogs that are practical. If they're in a bad situation, like stuck in a shelter with no one of his own, he'd just bide his time. He wouldn't kick at the traces. However, once he got where he knew things were good, then he'd let his lighter side show. Harold stared at me, like he was waiting to decide if he was biding his time a-wishing and a-hoping, or getting the good life.

And like a man who stares at the little stick with the plus sign on it, I knew the time for hypotheticals was over. "Come on, Harold. Let's go," and turned around matter-of-factly and walked toward the house. He perked right up and proceeded to plod right after me.

CC watched and said, "Well, how about that."

"Don't make fun of pack leader, dahlin'," I called over my shoulder. Still, she was happy and clasped hands together at her breast and sighed contentedly.

Opening the front door, Harold didn't try to scoot past me. *Whoozagootboy? Heezagootboy!* Calmly following me to the kitchen, he found himself a corner and laid down on the cool floor. I placed a bowl of water in front of him. "Here you go, Harold." He lapped it up then laid head on paws and went to sleep.

By this time Mom was making a pot of coffee and Dad was happily chompin' on a Dunkin' of his own. CC looked at me with those big eyes of hers and I said, "You done good." She smiled, crooked a finger at me to follow, and I did — straight to the car where she popped the trunk and we unloaded all of Harold's things. With that he was officially moved in and part of the family.

The next thing to do was to get his photograph. I snapped one of him sleeping. Then I said, "Harold." At his name, he opened one eye. Saw me putting on my walking shoes and popped right up, tail wagging. "Let's go, boy." Out the door we all went for walkies. He put his nose in the air, caught the scent of something, but decided it wasn't worth chasing. We walked to the performance shed with Harold scoping out the property and making wide, looping circles around us. When we went to cross the river, he stopped and stared like he'd died and gone to heaven. He jumped from the bridge straight into the water. Swam around a bit. Then climbed out on the shed side and shook himself dry.

Mom said, "I see your mudroom is gonna come in handy."

This whole time CC and I were snapping pictures like crazy and comparing shots. We finally made it to the shed where Dad showed Mom everything we'd been doing. Harold spied the horses and off he went, taking the long way around by swimming the river again, shaking himself, then running toward them. The horses watched him coming and met him at the fence. He popped under and they all proceeded to make introductions and got to playing.

CC and I looked at each other like proud parents because we were. Then I got a text from Misha.

    911! Come quick! 911!

I showed CC and she said Go! I took off running to the house to get car keys. When I got in the house, I called him, but there was no answer. Dang. I ran to the car and took off. The whole way over I continued to call, but still no answer.

Misha gets a delivery

I pulled up to Misha's house and heaved a huge sigh of relief. There he was. Sitting on his front steps. Calmly viewing my arrival like it was just another day. I screeched to a hard stop in his driveway, swung out the door, and ran toward him.

He waved. "Jaaaahhn."

"What's going on? What's the emergency?"

Misha stood and gave a typical Russian shrug. "You see. Come."

And in we went to the kitchen. Clutch was staring at me hard like I'd been cheating on him or something. He didn't roll over for his tummy rub like he usually did. Then I remembered I had a strange dog smell on me. But I didn't have time to worry about that right now because Misha was pointing to a big box sitting open on his table.

"This got delivered today."

We both understood the implications of the contents. There before us were fancy chocolate-dipped cookies — in shapes that wanted to look the same but were skewed randomly this way and that, therefore obviously not made in an automated bakery — and a bottle of wine. The handwritten note inside said *Paired for your dining pleasure. Hope you enjoy. Love your playing. Wanted to show my appreciation. Sincerely, Deb.*

"How many Deb's do you know, Misha?"

"Jaaahn, zees ees not frohm any Deb I know. Zees is from zee killer. Zee killer not sign real nahm. *Moy Bog na nebesakh!*"

"Oh, yeah. Right. What was I thinking?"

"What are you doooo*ink*?"

"I'm taking pictures, Misha. Do you have any latex gloves?"

"Goot idea. I get."

So while he went for the gloves, I was taking pictures of the outside of the box including the mailing label, any shipping barcodes or other labels, and handwriting. Didn't touch it or any of the contents with bare hands. Misha arrived with several pairs of latex gloves. We each put on two pair, then gingerly began getting pictures of how the contents were packed. To stabilize and protect them from shifting and breaking, sheets of newspaper had been stuffed all around and on top. We pulled those out and got pictures of the newspaper name and the publication date.

After all that was done, I logged onto Misha's WiFi and uploaded the pics to my Dropbox account and emailed them to myself and Misha. Then Detective Love got called.

"This is Detective Love," she answered.

"Hello, Detective. This is John Dann."

"Yes, Mr. Dann. How are you and the Asses today?"

"Not good. One of us just got a package."

"Who?"

"Misha Stefanuk. Homemade cookies and a bottle of wine was just delivered."

"Obviously you are suspicious of it or you wouldn't have called." There was silence for a moment then she said, "Okay. Don't touch anything. Where is this box now?"

"At Misha's house. We're both here."

"Okay. Address?"

So I gave her his address. She said she and her partner, Detective Mick (it was her nickname) Hepcutts, were coming over immediately to get it, but it would be at least two hours before they could get here. Not a problem, I said, we would not touch it. I texted CC and told her the outline of the situation and that it would be awhile before I got back. Now Misha and I had two hours to kill. What were we going to do? I hadn't brought Stella, so we couldn't rehearse.

Then I remembered Harold. "Meeeshah? You *wannnnah* see *peekchurs* of Harold?"

Misha stared at me hard. "Jaaaahhhn. Noomber one: Sooothurn Roooshun does not soond like zat. Noomber two:" — then he tried hard to get Southern on me — "who dee hayle is Hayrole?"

"Harold, Misha. Pronounced *hair uld*. Harold."

"Hayrrr old. Hayrrrold."

"Close enough. Anyway, glad you asked." And out I trotted the pictures of our new dog. "Okay, CC brought Harold home this morning. He's a rescue. An old lady died and the family didn't know what to do with it."

"Hayrrrold is dog name?"

"Yes, the old lady got the dog after her beloved husband died. Harold…get it?"

Misha nodded.

"Here's Harold sleeping in the kitchen."

"Heees beeg."

Swipe. "Here's Harold running across the bridge." Swipe. "Here's Harold jumping in the river." Swipe. "See?" Swipe. "Ain't he cute?"

"*Aaaahhh*. Heeees haffing a goot time."

"Yes!" Swipe. "Here's Harold shaking himself dry." Swipe. "Here's Harold running to meet the horses." Swipe. "That's it."

"Why no more?"

"You called, that's why."

"Yesss. Hey, maybe I bring Cloootch when I come over."

"That is a great idea." I looked over at Clutch, who was laying with his back to me. "I see Clutch smells Harold and is jealous."

"Poor Cloootch. Cooom here, boy." Clutch slunk over and put his head in Misha's lap for some loving, but gave me the stink eye.

And so ten minutes passed and we went outside to sit on the porch and settled in to enjoy the sun. Clutch finally seemed to forgive me. I could tell because he slunk over and slowly rolled onto his back, tentatively lifting a leg as if to say "You'll still give me belly rubs, right?" And I rubbed his belly which, in dog language, meant "Of course, you cute little son of a bitch you. We're still good."

"You now forgiven, Jaaaahhn."

"Yezzz I am." I bent down to Clutch and took his head in my hands and scratched his ears. "Whooozagootboy? Youzzagootboy! Yezzzz you are." Clutch agreed with me.

And thus time passed and before too long here came Detectives Charlene Love and Mick Hepcutts. Love popped the trunk and she and Mick dug around and came out with evidence bags from small to very large.

We watched them walk toward us. "Mr. Dann. You remember Detective Mick Hepcutts?"

"Yes, ma'am, I do. How are you?" Mick nodded and held up the bags. I introduced them to Misha. "This is Misha Stefanuk. The box and items are in the kitchen."

Misha led the way with Clutch hot on his heels. I held the door for the ladies; I am a good Southern boy. And in we all tramped up the stairs and to the right where a beam of sunshine was pouring in a window like a spotlight on the possible evidence.

"I thought I told you not to touch it," Love snapped.

"We didn't touch it…after it was opened. But until it was opened Misha didn't know what it was."

She stared hard at me. "Did you touch it?"

I could not lie. "Yes, but only with latex gloves."

"I thought I told you not to touch it!" she snapped again.

"After we called you we didn't touch it again."

Love and Hepcutts shook their heads as if to say civilians, and took evidence away.

Now it was time to get home for the Test Jam and also see how Harold was doing.

Test Jam, prep, tour, and a plan

The Test Jam was a big success if by big success you meant we found out what didn't work and what needed to be rejiggered, improved, or had been forgotten. But everybody who came knew it was a testing of the facilities and so they did their best to strain the limits.

Joe's students came as did a few of Misha's, along with music teachers in surrounding schools and some of their students, too. Word had gotten round. Parents brought blankets. Some dads fell asleep on blankets waiting for their kids. A few moms enjoyed chatting with other moms.

Dad was there, too. He kept a list of everything that needed to be worked on. I was unhappy with how much was still needed to be done as I thought I'd given it a lot of thought and was on top of it all. On the other hand, Dad thought there wasn't much that needed to be attended to and was very happy. I guess that meant our expectations were different, because the list didn't change, only our opinion of it.

In any case, lots of excitement came out of the event. Some music teachers from local schools thought it was a great place to be able to have more concerts in an affordable fashion and were asking for rates and contracts. Dad put that on the list and I said I'd have that to them before very long.

Misha and I spent the next few days preparing for our annual swing through the Southern states of Georgia, Florida, and Alabama. This time the tour would be five days, five venues, seven shows, and lots of miles to and from the Florida-Alabama line to Jacksonville to Savannah and back home. Clutch would stay with CC and Harold, which got CC all excited about Harold having play dates. What in the heck was a play date?

The day before we were to leave on Friday, Misha came over. We got The Van cleaned, gear packed, blankets, pillows, sheets put on the bunks, plenty of snack food. Personal items would go in tomorrow. Misha stayed for dinner and left around eight. CC and I took a late-evening walk to The Barn, The Shed, and back around. Harold, looping circles around us and visiting with the steeds, met us back at the house just as we were getting there.

It was time to take a shower and proceeded to do so, but darn I forgot to get myself a towel and washcloth and so hollered for help. "Ceeee-Ceeee! Can you bring me a washcloth and towel?"

And she did. Except she delivered them in a pile on the rug in front of the shower door. Of course, I didn't see that right away because the door was fogged up and I had soap in my eyes, but I heard the door open. By the time I rinsed my face I heard, "Need some help washing your back, big boy?"

Well, he-e-e-e-ellOOO there! Thank goodness I had put some of those sticky things on the shower floor that help feet to grip otherwise we would've been in a hurtin' heap and that just would not do. Come to find out I really didn't need a towel after all and we dove headlong into the bed and under the covers where we…let me just put it this way: I gave her something to remember me by while I was gone. Then we slept.

"Harold! Sheesh!" I hollered. Let me tell you, there ain't anything as cold as a dog's nose poking where it don't need to be. "Get." CC rolled my way and before too long I had something to remember her by while I was gone.

Finally up and dressed, CC headed out the door to work just as Misha pulled up with Clutch. The recording room was closed up tight. We let the dogs have a final run, put out some water and food for them in the kitchen, said goodbye. I locked the house, we stowed our last personal items.

"OK, let's get a pic of us in front of The Van," I said, and pointed at Misha's phone. He took the pic and off we went heading toward Alabama. As soon as we were on the paved road, Misha posted the pic, captioned it "Tour starts!", and tagged me. We fell silent then. Just two boys on our own. Which is not often a good thing.

"Jaaahn. I haf idea."

The sun was blaring into my eyes. "Open the glove box there and hand me my sun cheaters." He did. "That's better. So, what's the idea?"

"You know box had tracking noomber on it?"

"Yeah, I saw that."

"Can't thoss be traced?"

"Hang on. Do you mean can law enforcement trace the tracking number back to the person who sent it? Like, okay, what if the sender wanted to get notified of delivery and stupidly put in their real email address?"

"Yessss! Ooooh. Don't think will happen. She's too smart."

"Right. Though I bet Detective Love would tell you that criminals make stupid mistakes all the time, so it's possible and we can only hope."

We rode for another twenty miles in silence. Both thinking. Not about the same thing, though. I was thinking of CC's going away present this morning, but the revery was interrupted.

"Jaaaahn. Let's flooosh out zee sender."

"How?"

"We know eees someone we know, *pravil'no?*"

"Right."

"So, I possst on Facebuuk about tour. And-and-and," he was getting excited, "also zee package with coooookies and wine and how we take with us in The Van. Then you comment about —"

"I comment about how I can't wait to have some of it!"

"*Da! Da!* Zen zee who likes and comments."

"Yeah! And we post some of the pictures we took of the contents!"

Misha screamed and I threw on the brakes. "What?" I screamed back, not seeing any cars too close to us.

"I got stuuuung by beeeee."

"Where?"

He turned his face toward me. His right cheek had a red welt on it and it hurt if his moaning was any indication. He scraped at the spot to get the stinger out. He finally got it out by the time I pulled off at the next exit with a QuikTrip. He got a small cup and put ice in it and stuffed his pocket with a wad of napkins. I got coffee. He bought Benadryl and a Coke. Then we were on the road again.

We had a show tonight, so Misha was trying his best to keep the swelling down with ice and the drug. The Benadryl put him to sleep. I only found that out when I heard his head hit the window and the ice hit the floor. I grabbed the Coke before it went, screwed on the top, and put it in a cup holder. "You're welcome, buddy."

Three hours later it was time to stop for food. Misha woke up hard when I rolled into a Cracker Barrel. "Come on. Let's get food in you. Something for the Benadryl to gnaw on for awhile. You got to be sharp for the show."

Misha stretched his neck, rolled his head around. "Where are we?"

"Montgomery."

"How long I sleep?"

"Almost three hours."

We went in. Misha went to the bathroom to wash his face. I got a table, ordered coffee, then began studying the menu. By the time my mind was made up, here came Misha, dragging his poor ol' self over and flopping into a chair.

"Whatcha wanna drink?" the waitress said to Misha as she laid down packets with spoons, forks, and knives, and slapped a handful of napkins between us after which she placed a hot cup and a pile of creamers in front of me.

He pointed at my coffee.

"Okay, baby. Another coffee. Y'all know whatcha gonna eat?"

"I'll have the Sunrise Sampler with hash brown casserole. And put the sawmill gravy in its own little bowl and make it real hot."

"One Sunrise, hash browns, hot gravy on the side. Got it." She turned to Misha. "You ready, sweetie?"

He pointed.

"One bowl of frosted flakes and orange juice. Coming up. I'll be back with your coffee in a jif, baby."

"Let me see your cheek." Misha pulled his hand away and turned the cheek toward me. "You won't look like too much of a freak onstage. How's it feel?"

"Still hurts."

When the waitress brought Misha's coffee and cream, I asked if she would be willing to take a picture of us when our food was delivered. She said, as I knew she would, "Sure, baby." About fifteen minutes later, we'd had a fill up and our food was coming out the kitchen door.

"Give me your phone, baby." I did. Misha and I got posed so that the food would show. Misha leaned on his hurt cheek so it wouldn't show too much. She snapped the pic, handed back the phone, and winked before she headed to the next table.

"Okay…Gonna post this now…You. Are. Tagged. What we gonna say?"

Misha crunched on frosted flakes and thought. He tilted his head back to keep food in his mouth and said through it all, "On zee road again making music wiss friends."

"Brilliant." Thumbs went flying. "Done." Remember, they don't call me Adman for nothing. "Here, Misha. Eat some protein." I shared a sausage patty with him, then dug in and enjoyed every bite.

Within a half hour, we were back in The Van and getting on I-65, just quiet. Not yakking like we usually do, when Misha hollered. "*Syr i krekery*!"

I almost jumped out the window and hollered, "You get stung again?"

"No!"

"Then why did you holler Siri crack?"

He was digging out his phone and scrolling through apps until he found Facebook. He stopped. "Eees not Siri crack. I said *syr i krekery* which means cheese and crackers. I not want say curse, so I say *syr i krekery*." Then he held up his phone for me to see as I drove. "*My zabyli podlost'*."

Now, you need to understand that Misha is my best friend and so, while I do not speak Russian as you well know, sometimes our minds our totally sympatico and no translation is ever needed. This was not one of those times. Again, my expression must've shown it. "Translation?"

"*My zabyli podlost'*. We forget sneaky."

"Sneaky? Oh! Oh-oh. Yeah."

"I do now." And so Misha spent the next few minutes posting about the wonderful gift of wine and cookies he got from a friend, but he did not tag in the post the person whose name was on the package because, as we all know, she wasn't the one who sent them. It was the killer who sent them and we did not yet know who that was.

We went southwest until we hit State Road 29, took a left, heading due south and straight to the Flora-Bama for two shows tonight. An early short show, more as a warmup and system testing, then the main show starting at eleven. Tickets were sold out for both and dinner and drinks were included for us.

We arrived just as one of the four owners was driving out of the parking lot. "Adman! Misha!" Joe called out. "Pat's inside. I'll be back later. Got some stuff to do. See you for the late show."

We waved back at him and parked where we could unload easily. Misha proceeded to pull gear from the van while I went inside hunting up Pat to find out where he wanted us to set up. Pat saw me coming and waved me over with a crooked finger that said *follow me*. I did. Upon arriving at the stage, he pointed.

Out I went to help Misha with pack mule duty. Didn't take us long to get our gear in and set up and a quick sound check. We grabbed two Bushwackers, a drink they are famous for. You outta go and try it sometimes. Anyway, of course before we went to the beach we had to get pictures of us together with Pat and holding up the famous drink. We headed to the beach to chill out.

"Okay, Misha. What we gonna say about this?"

Misha held up a finger for me to wait because he had a brain freeze from sucking on the frozen concoction too fast. Then he came up with a one-liner. "Beeeesh, Booosh Whackers, and baebbs."

"Yeah. You can say that. I can't."

"*Akh, da.* CC no like that," he grinned. "Okay. How about, uhhh, beeeesh and Boooosh Whackers at Flora-Bama. Come out for zee uuuummm—"

"Got it." Thumbs flew again. "Done. You're tagged."

Misha laughed and pulled out his phone and shared the post saying something about babes. I remembered those days fondly, but not as fondly as the days with CC. Honestly, it was all big talk for Misha these days, he was so over women at this point in time. Too much wasted time and too much to do artistically was what he'd been saying of late.

We watched over the next few days as everybody, except anybody on our list of possible killers, gave Misha grief about getting fan-girled over and then somebody posted, "Whoever sent it had to know you well enough to know where you live." A winking emoji was inserted at the end.

Anyway, that set off another round of teasing Misha about women, and keeping his friends in the dark about them, and other such things as boys will say to boys about girls.

Days two thru five of tour

The owners of the Flora-Bama know their customers well. The honky-tonk had been in business in Pensacola, Florida, since 1964. They do oysters, drinks, and music with equal parts cool and style and ease. I'd been doing shows there with Misha and some others for several years. We had a very good professional relationship with them. They trusted us to show up. We trusted them to pay correctly and timely. We were in the main room on this trip.

Sold a decent amount of merch (T-shirts with both me and Misha on the front, CDs, and easy-to-autograph vinyl). Before the night was over, certain of the babes had already cut, twisted, and tied some of those shirts in ways that highlighted their assets, natural or otherwise, to great effect. I had to waggle my wedding band at a few and shake my head no-no-no. One young lady wouldn't give up and so I said, "Look. I'll happily do ya, but my wife and I have a deal. You have to call her from your phone and first pass the test to get permission."

She wasn't that drunk that she took me up on it. She turned to Misha with a sloppy ogle. He frowned and said, "Go-a-way."

A couple of singers came in. Even though this was not an open jam, we knew them and they added fun to the night. In between sets we caught up with them. Lot of fun. Good to see them.

John, one of the owners, called us over to the bar after the last show. "Great night, guys. Listen, instead of sleeping in your van, why don't you come sleep at my house? Extra bedrooms and nobody's sleeping in them tonight, so come on."

Misha and I looked at each other, brains totally sympatico, no translation needed. "Thanks for the offer, John, but we are so hyped up, it's gonna take several hours for us to come down. We're just gonna hit the road and sleep when we get tired."

"Okay. Next time, Adman. I'll send the money to the same address, right? I mean, I heard you bought some farm so wasn't sure…"

"Got married and bought sixty acres. We board horses. I'm building a performance shed, and I've got a recording studio all tricked out. Money still goes to the PO Box."

"Ten-four." He chuckled. "You're gonna be hosting tours before you know it, man."

We all laughed at that. "Please, God, I hope so. Tell Joe, Pat, and Cam we said goodbye and we'll talk later."

"Will do. Later, Misha!" With a wave, he turned on his heel and went to shut down for the night.

We climbed into The Van around three a.m., and pushed east toward Jacksonville and the MOJO Kitchen, BBQ Pit & Blues Bar in a five-plus hour drive. Hyped as we were after any performance, we talked nonstop. Let me put it another way. Misha talked nonstop and I mostly just yelled things like Yeah! and Hell yeah! and I agree! and You're right!, laughing like a crazy banshee at Misha's way of telling a story, only occasionally breaking in with a Shut up, I've got a story! and Let me finish, geez!

By five we were both too tired to talk. By six we were feeling the need to sleep, so we pulled in to an all-night truck stop off the highway featuring a homestyle restaurant and shower facilities, found a parking space, and climbed into our racks. I woke around twelve to Misha talking in his sleep. Thank goodness it was all in Russian as I didn't want to even know what secrets he was spilling. I got my kit out and rented a shower. A few minutes later I heard "Jaaaahn!"

"I'm here, Misha."

"Okay. I get shoooowher."

The stall had a mirror riveted to the wall; that was helpful when it came to shaving. I dried and dressed in fresh clothes and left the stall. "Misha! See you in the restaurant."

Okay! echoed off the tiles. Five minutes later, bag stowed, I was at a table perusing the menu. Meatloaf, real mashed potatoes and, what looked like to me, fresh green beans were a prominent feature on just about every table. Must be delicious.

I'd been thinking of ordering a salad with some sort of chicken on it, but the meatloaf just looked so darn good. Heard Misha talking, so looked up. He was at the far end of the restaurant and had stopped to talk to total strangers. Misha was good at that. By the time he was heading my way, the whole table was laughing.

"What was that all about?"

"Man T-shirt with sumpsink...*smeshnoy*...errr...foooneee."

I nodded. "Meatloaf dinner looks good."

A young fella came to take our orders. He was back in an efficient manner with our drinks and a basket of hot rolls and tiny tubs of honey butter. Five minutes later, out came our plates. Dang it was good, but there was so much I couldn't eat it all, so I got a to-go container and took it with me. Misha took his turn driving. Ding-ding-ding went my phone. Texts with pictures from CC showing Harold settling in on The Farm and playing with the horses and —

What the heck?

Harold sleeping on my side of the bed with Clutch, all snuggled up with CC? Oh, heck no.

Just let me tell you a thing or two right now. When I get home, that is gonna change. I am not sleeping with no dang dog and I don't care what you think of me about that.

Two hours into the last three of the trip to Jacksonville, I was digging in the back for the rest of the meatloaf with gravy and rolls, still lukewarm, resuming my chomp all the way through it. Dang it was good.

I had no sooner finished than Misha said, "You know we play at BBQ tonight?"

"Don't you worry. I'll be hungry again."

"Yes, you will. I wonder how Clutch is doing?"

"I'll text CC and find out." Her one word answer was `Fine!` followed by a picture of Harold and Clutch frolicking in the wide river. I showed it to Misha then forwarded to him. Then I showed him Clutch on my bed.

"Cloootch is sleeping with a woman. More than I've been doing lately."

"That will stop when I get home. I am not sleeping with a dog."

Misha smiled. It was a knowing smile. He shrugged and chuckled.

"What does that mean?"

He smiled again. "It means *znamenityye posledniye slova* — fahmoos lass words."

"What does that mean?"

"You weel fin' oot."

Enough of that conversation. I changed the topic. "We forgot to get a picture at the truckstop."

"Dang." Then he laughed. "Take a picture of the empty box."

So I did. Then cross-posted it to Instagram, Facebook, and MeWe with this: "Meatloaf with gravy and taters and beans. Sorry. Ate it all. But, hey, Jacksonville fans should come out to tonight's show at MOJO Kitchen, BBQ Pit & Blues Bar. 9:00 pm." Then I settled back and listened to the iPhone Maps app tell Misha where to go. When we were about ten miles out, I called the venue to talk to the night manager, told him we were close, and got instructions for where to unload and park.

We unloaded and setup, then headed to the beach for some sun. I like the ocean on the East Coast better than the Gulf. Waves are bigger and in a storm much wilder. Rain started, so found a bar with shelter that opened to the shore and enjoyed the view for awhile before heading to the venue.

The gig went fine. Only had to waggle my wedding ring once. This venue was favored by bikers, though most of those just enjoyed dressing up as that for the weekends then heading back to Mommy and Daddy roles and jobs by Monday morning. It didn't matter because they sure did like their leather. Misha had a couple of real biker chicks twisting beers above their heads, and giving him the eye. He paid them no mind but nodded to the owners of the backseats the women rode on. Misha knows when to show respect so as not to get a beatdown put on him. We got a few requests, most in the Jazz genre and fulfilled those.

But this crowd also liked their "Freebird", or "Free Bird" if you like. For those who don't know, "Free Bird" is a power ballad performed by American rock band Lynyrd Skynyrd and first released on their 1973 debut album. Power ballads usually start slow then build in intensity with drums, electric guitars, and, every now and then, choirs. What made this one different from other power ballads was its length at nine minutes and eight seconds, plus the variety of sections and the seamless musical movement between them. No section could be left out without affecting the whole. Sure, there is a four minute and forty-one second radio version but all it does is tease and make listeners mad they aren't getting the whole thing.

Fans of Lynyrd Skynyrd, longtime and new, love hollering the title of the song at just about every live music show they come to. That has come to be anathema to bands, many of whom get mad at the audience and let them know they don't appreciate being asked to play it, often acting insulted that they should be asked as if it's below them or something. Granted, there is a time and a place to fulfil that request, but geez, if a musician or a band wants to make fans outside of their established genre, learning the song and doing it their way is a good way to make the band or musician memorable.

When I was fifteen, Dad took me to a concert of a Jazz trumpeter I wanted to hear. It was great. I was studying the whole show and the band. Then some guy in the back hollered *FREEBIRD!* Some folks laughed, others groaned. Somebody hollered *SHUT UP!* But not the band. They grinned at each other. The drummer shrugged. And when the opening notes came out of the horn, the audience applauded and settled in to listen. Fifteen minutes later, I kid you not, the band owned that song because they did it their way. In homage to the song, they still didn't give up their Jazz roots and had worked in homages to other Jazz favorites in the style of "Freebird". I learned a lot that night both musically and how to engage an audience. Never forgot those lessons.

So when the drunk guy in the back hollered the same and the audience applauded his choice, Misha and I proceeded to fulfill his request. And let me tell you, you ain't never heard "Free Bird" like a Russian Jazz musician with heavy Classical roots can play it. In any case, everybody enjoyed the show and, oh yeah, we sold some merch. *Ka! Ching!*

This sort of thing went on for the rest of the tour. The Van earned her keep, we made a profit, venue owners were happy, and sold more merch. Same story. Different city. Between gigs, though… when we had nothing to occupy our time and minds…we wondered how to catch a killer. Sure, we knew Detective Love was working on it. She did not know our little community as well as we did, so we had an idea and set to work on it. We would be back home sometime Wednesday.

It was time for the Amateur Sleuth Society to get together again. So, on Sunday, while we were in Savannah, I sent texts to the guys with a picture attached of the bottles of wine that came in the box to Misha. It said

```
Thursday my house same time beer pizza
can somebody see who sells this wine?
```

Ding-ding-ding-da-ding-a-ding-ding came back in quick succession with thumbs-up emojis.

The longest, sweetest mile

Arriving home is always a good thing. Covered by every major singer there was back in the day, there's an old song that goes "The longest mile, the sweetest mile you'll ever roam is the last mile home." "The Longest Mile" was written in 1949 by Walter Kent, composer of "I'll Be Home for Christmas" and "(There'll Be Bluebirds Over) The White Cliffs of Dover", and songwriter and arranger Walton Farrar.

I can definitely attest to the truthfulness of the sentiment because that last mile before The Van, Misha, and I hit my driveway was as long as the almost twelve hundred we'd covered the previous few days. I texted CC we were a mile out to give her a head's up on our arrival.

There they were. CC, Harold, and Clutch. All three waiting on us, tails just a-wagging. CC threw herself on me. Clutch threw himself on Misha. And Harold was barking, circling us all until he finally pushed himself between CC and me to get him some loving. Harold loved it when I said, "Who's a good boy? Youzza good boy. Yessssyouare-yessss!"

As Clutch and Harold had one last romp, we got Misha's stuff transferred to his vehicle and waved goodbye to them, then unloaded The Van and got all my gear and such squared away. CC's tail was still just a-wagging and when she started begging, don't you know the outro to James Brown's "It's a Man's World" popped into mind: Man needs a woman, otherwise he's lost in the wilderness, in bitterness, and loneliness.

That longest mile is made the sweeter with just such receptions as this. I'm a blessed man…and not about to forget it, either. The evening went on in quite the satisfactory fashion and you know what I mean by that. We fell asleep in each other's arms. No, Harold was not in the bed with us and yes, he was on the floor. Anyway, it sure felt good to sleep on a real mattress, too.

Around one-thirty, Harold's snoring woke me up. I had not realized Harold snored, too. Unlike CC's snoring which was kind of cute, Harold's wasn't. In fact, it was so obnoxious it woke me up with a shock.

So, blood pumping and mind racing, I got up and went to the living room to watch some *MeTV* because late at night it has all kinds of great shows from when every man dressed in ties and suit jackets to chase bad guys or fight good guys. When bespoke suit jackets matched pants, like Mannix, or rack-bought didn't match, like Cannon. Maybe cravats were worn, like Barnaby Jones did sometimes, and bad guys spoke with classy accents and had naïve, good-hearted but talented dames run their errands resulting in somebody's gonna die.

Yep, it's a man's world for sure, and here I was, thick in the middle of a chase for a killer and not one matching private eye suit and tie in sight. This would have to be remedied.

So there I was, in the dark room lit only by the TV, laying on the sofa wrapped in a blanket, when I again woke with a start because a cold nose had managed to find its way under the blanket plunking itself smack on my warm personal property. I yelped and flinched wide awake and there it went, the remote control flying up in the air.

"Harold!" I hollered.

Harold just stared back at me, but I saw the twinkle in his grin even as his eyes rolled up at me sadly, head hung, and tail brushing the floor that said *Izzagoodboy, right?*

I hope-hope-hoped the remote was close enough to reach from the warmth of my cocoon, but of course it wasn't. So, my feet hit the cool floor, but the remote had come apart and I couldn't find all the pieces. Flipping the light on, I found front and back and battery and put it all back together. Then, trying it out to see if it worked, found there was still one corner to snap all the way down. Curse-curse-curse-snap-try and it worked. Wide awake again, it was back to the sofa and the blanket. Curse-curse-curse-jump-up-turn-off-light, jump back to the sofa. Where the heck's the remote?

By this time, wide awake, I thought of a snarky witticism to put on FB about Harold and his cold, cold surprise in the dark. A half-hour later, eyes heavy, I left the office, got snuggled back in bed, and what do I hear? Only Cannon's booming voice warning a bad guy to *Drop it!* and then remember the TV is still on. Big sigh. How I wish I had The Clapper. Drag my sorry, sad boohiney out of the bed back to the living room, but cannot find the remote. Crap. Where is it? Dang it, it's in my office on the computer desk. I pad my way to get it, and return to shut off the TV.

But wait, as they say on infomercials, there's more! Cannon is just ending and Barnaby Jones is getting ready to start and "OHMYGOD, I'VE NEVER SEEN THAT ACTOR SO YOUNG!"

So there I am, wide awake again...happily so this time because HOLY COW look at all those big-name actors and actresses in bit parts. So that's where they got started. They're just so skinny and fresh-faced. Not a facelift among them and not one soft-focus lens pointed their way, either. An hour later, just as Barnaby Jones is ending, I reach for the remote to turn off the TV, but can't find it. So I fan the blankets and there it goes clattering across the floor again.

I finally made it back to bed and fell asleep. An instant later, or so it seemed, CC's alarm went off and our Thursday officially began. Stumbling to the bathroom and wiping steam from the mirror, my bleary eyes can barely focus, but I heard the shower turn off and the curtain yank open and suddenly I could see clearly.

Handing a towel to CC, she didn't notice I had miraculously regained my sight, and she simply said thank you and began to dry herself off in a functional fashion. As if she was not impressed with what she was drying off.

"Baby? Can I help you with that?"

She paused and looked up. "Help with what?"

Ain't she just the cutest ever? "You know, baby. Drying your back and such as that."

"No. I have to get to work." That was blunt and my feelings were hurt. I was just trying to be, you know, helpful. But then she made it all better. "If you even come near me Imma gonna hafta jump yer bones and then I'll be late for work and that just will not do. Now, get out of here so I can get ready."

I gave her a couple of salutes that made her take a deep breath or two and waggle her eyebrows, and one ma'am-yes-ma'am that made her laugh before pointing me out the door. Yanking on a pair of shorts, I headed to the kitchen to brew coffee and prepare breakfast. Thirty minutes later she was gone. Harold was let out and, without a look back, he took off like a shot toward the field for his morning visit with the horses.

Harold and the horses are like a Jazz band made up of people speaking different languages. In their case, it was barks and neighs, but somehow they found a way to communicate. Like Jazz, a hidden language that is known in the soul.

Harold took the long way around, flapping his tongue and letting out short sharp barks in E flat, of all things, the whole time letting *equus caballus* know he was on his way. Distant hooves beat a rhythm toward their regular meeting spot.

Commence to begin to plan to flush out a killer

Harold, who had already come back for a nap after his field romp, smelled the pizza before I even heard the car. He was standing at attention at the door and I didn't know why. So, just as I was finishing with marketing and phone calls, I heard a car pull up. By the time I got to the door it opened and in walked Misha with Chip. So it was two cars that pulled up simultaneously. Misha carried beer. After one sniff at the cans, Harold ignored Misha and proceeded to go make friends with Chip who was toting pizza.

"Do not give Harold any pizza. Gives him the farts, bad." However, I was hungry and didn't even stand on ceremony. No plate for me. Just a slice in hand. Misha popped a top and set it in front of me. I mumbled thanks through a mouthful of pizza, threw paper plates on the table, then the doorbell rang and in walked André, Gerry, and Leland. More pizza and beer were slung on the table, and eatin' and talkin' and burpin' commenced — and yes some boohiney-tootin', too — as we waited.

I got a text from Ty saying they were five minutes out. *They* being Carl, Arturo, and David.

I reiterated my warning about pizza and dog gas stinkin'. Harold, still giving the hangdog look at anybody holding a slice, finally got some sneaked to him. I knew this because he must've slid real quiet under the table to eat it. I watched him slide out real quiet still picking at his teeth with his tongue.

"Who fed Harold?"

André had who-me-guilty on his face and I gave him a dirty look and he said, "I didn't give it to him." Pointing at Harold. "He stole it."

Harold, knowing he was caught when he heard me holler "Harold! Outside with you!", was already heading toward the door. He didn't care. He'd had him a slice and that was all that mattered. Tail wagging, he wasn't even pretending to be sorry. I slammed the door behind his pizza-stealing ass. Hopefully, the farts would be over before bedtime.

Leland, ever the organizer, was cleaning up the mess, consolidating pizza slices and throwing away empty boxes and cans. He said, "Let's get this show on the road."

With that, everybody put their game faces on. It was time to hatch a plan to catch a killer.

"I think," David began, "that we had been talking about throwing a party and inviting the two we think are the killers. Faith and Roxanne. Right?" We nodded. "So, shouldn't we get a date for that set right now?"

"What if the killer has already been caught? Have you heard from the detectives?"

"No, haven't heard. So no news is bad news and we just keep looking for the killer."

So, we spent the next half hour working out the date and found that we could all make it two weeks from now. A Thursday evening. We were each tasked with inviting both Faith and Ro-Ro. Misha was tasked with putting out a post on his timeline that would stir the killer's pot…that is, if Facebook actually showed the post. Thus the additional need for everybody to text friends and send invites.

I texted everybody the time, date, place, and address with a link that would work in Maps or in a GPS system on whatever phone they had. I sent all that via email to myself because I had a feeling I might ought to invite Detectives Love and Hepcutts, too. They would need to come undercover so as not to scare off the killer.

"I want as many people here as possible. But remember: Nobody knows except us — and CC and the detectives, of course — what we're up to."

Gerry, big smile on his face, piped up with a question. "What do we bring, if anybody should ask?"

"Tell everybody that the Adman is cooking out burgers and hot dawgs and we'll have all the fixin's and drinks, including beer and wine. It's a party! Bring instruments if they want."

"Hey, does this mean we'll be having the party at The Shed?"

"Misha, that's a good idea, but I don't know. I'll give it some thought. Hey, anybody have big plastic or metal tubs they can bring to hold ice?"

Three hands raised. "Great. I will leave you three to take care of that, then. Okay. So. That brand of wine that was sent to Misha. Did anybody find out where it is sold?"

"I did," Carl said.

"Great. Can you get one bottle the same size and labeling as the picture I'm sending you now?"

Ding! "Got it. Sure. I can."

"Misha, make sure you get that from Carl before you come so that it looks like you are carrying it in."

Misha held up a beer can over his head and said, "Yes, I weel make beeg entry holding oop zee bottle of wine." He pranced around demonstrating his beeg entry technique.

Then Arturo started laughing. "Who's gonna hold the spotlight against the back of that bottle?"

We all stared at him because we didn't get it.

"You know. Like Hitchcock used to do in his movies to make the poisoned bottle of liquid look spookier? Easier to follow along when watching?"

Oh, we all said together, right. We laughed along with him, but then we all got serious. To-do's in hand, the guys left. A killer was on the loose. Who would be next?

Good question. The other murders, and the attempt on Misha, had come in quick succession, but were the victims limited to four? We hadn't heard of any other deaths in our Atlanta Jazz community. Maybe the fact that Misha was not yet dead was adding a level of anticipatory intensity to her game and that's why she had not sent any poison to anybody else.

Like an old Jazz man I knew, Johnny Knapp who died of old age not too long ago, told me one time years ago. He said, "John, an audience will forgive you for playing a wrong note. They will forgive you for forgetting the words. But if you get the timing wrong, they will kick you off the stage."

Our killer probably understood that lesson, and so, like in music where timing is everything, the timing of her kills was very important to her. There was a meaning there that only she knew, obviously.

My to-do was to let CC know of the party date, make a list of food and drink to purchase, and charcoal and so forth, and to also call Detective Love. I was not looking forward to that call. Thoroughly convinced Love would try to stop me from having the party, I was gonna have to tell her I'd do it anyway, no matter what. I dialed. Heard it ringing. Then —

LOVE: Detective Love speaking.

ADMAN: Hello, Detective Love. This is John Dann, the saxo—

LOVE: Yes. I remember. Has somebody else died?

ADMAN: Not that I am aware of. However, I wanted to let you know that…uhhh…ummm, The Amateur Sleuth Society —

LOVE [growing displeasure]: What are the A.S.S.'s up to now?

ADMAN: Now, don't get mad until you hear the whole plan?

LOVE: Plan! You've made a plan?

ADMAN: Now, hang on. Just hang on and let me explain what we're doing.

LOVE [big sigh]: Continue.

ADMAN: We're going to throw a party and you and Detective Hepcutts are invited.

LOVE: A party?

ADMAN: Yes, two Thursdays from now. Fourteen days away. My place. I will text you the address.

LOVE: We've already been there. Hang on. I'm putting you on speakerphone. [Clunking noises.] Detective Hepcutts is now listening in.

HEPCUTTS: I am here.

ADMAN: Hello, Detective. So you two come to the party but you have to be undercover. I mean, you can't show up flashing your badges, looking all official and such as that. The Amateur Sleuth Society has narrowed down the list of possible perps to two. They are both invited. We are

going to trick them by having Misha bring that
bottle of wine to the party.

LOVE: [shouting] We cannot let you have that bottle
of wine. It is poisoned.

HEPCUTTS [groaning]: Are you stupid?

ADMAN: No. I'm not stupid. And I know we can't
use the actual bottle of wine. We will buy a
lookalike bottle and pretend it is the one.

LOVE: Oh.

ADMAN: Then we'll attempt to share it with the
two possibles and see who declines.

HEPCUTTS: That's not a bad plan.

LOVE: And then what?

ADMAN: I don't know, but isn't that helpful
somehow? By the way, you say the wine was
poisoned?

LOVE: Yes. Tremetol. In both the wine and the
cookies. And not just little doses either. Enough
to kill a horse and a cow if they shared the lot.
So, if Misha had drank that wine and eaten
those cookies, he'd have been dead pretty quick.

HEPCUTTS: It's closely related to poison hemlock.
That's the plant that killed Socrates. Comes from

a plant called white snakeroot with clusters of small white flowers. The plant contains the toxic alcohol known as tremetol.

ADMAN: Is there a cure if found out early enough?

LOVE: There is no cure. Once ingested, death will eventually occur. The only thing that can be done is to just make the victim more comfortable.

ADMAN: Eventually? How long does it take to kill somebody?

HEPCUTTS: Anywhere from two to ten days. Lots of abdominal pain. Super thirsty. Vomiting. And that's just for starters. Get shaky and trembly. Then constipation. Can't eat. Get weak and can't stand or walk. Then you can't use any muscles, nothing will work together. Before long, coma. Then death.

LOVE: Guess who died of tremetol poisoning in 1818? Abraham Lincoln's mother, Nancy Hanks Lincoln, that's who.

ADMAN: Somebody murdered Abraham Lincoln's mother?

LOVE: No, see back then with the migratory move across the continent, white snakeroot grew everywhere and lots of people who didn't know about it thought it would make a great tea or cooked the greens or something. I don't know how they ingested it, but they did. Thousands died from it. Also, cows and horses ate it and died, too.

ADMAN: That sounds like a pretty bad way to die.

LOVE: It is. We've got permission from the families to exhume the three bodies of…

HEPCUTTS: Barry Lamon. Mario Mireles. And…

LOVE: Angela Peterson. They will look for a broad spectrum of poisons, of course, since, you know, just because Misha's wine and cookies were laced with white snakeroot doesn't mean that was used in all instances. They will definitely test for tremetol.

ADMAN: Okay. That sounds great. So, can y'all come to the party?

LOVE: Are you sure you want to do this? I can't stop you from doing it. I mean, I'd do it if it were me, but I'm a professional bad-guy-getter. You're just an amateur.

ADMAN: Detective Love. Detective Hepcutts. That's why we want you there. Please, please say you can come.

LOVE [long silence]: Yes, we will be there. If anything, just to stop you from doing something really stupid.

We said goodbye, that is, they hung up on me as I was saying goodbye, but then I got to thinking. I thought Misha should already have the bottle open and part of it already imbibed. Then the killer, seeing the bottle partially empty would think the poison had been delivered.

I couldn't wait to tell Misha that he would have a beeg entry on the stage that was our party. He was gonna love it. I dialed his number and gave him the extra details. Oh yeah. He was excited about his starring role.

These next two weeks were gonna crawl by, I just knew it.

Let's get this party started

I was wrong. Two weeks flew past. Besides everything I usually did — gigs, lessons, and jams — Harold managed to get himself in a skunk fight and lose. He came whizz-banging out of the woods making a beeline for home, howling all the way. We thought he'd been bit and in he ran straight to the kitchen where he proceeded to stink up the joint.

"Harold! Out!"

He was not a happy camper, but we got him outside and, while CC was looking up on the Internet what to do about skunk spray, I was running a bath in a big old metal tub up at the barn. Thank goodness Harold loves water and jumped in, dunking his face right smack in the water, and thus flushing out his eyes. After a few minutes of that, his eyes weren't near as red. Then here came CC, hot-footing it our way. She had a big plastic bottle of something she'd mixed up.

"What's that?" I asked.

"Supposedly this will help clean off the oily spray and will help deactivate the smell. It's two quarts of water, two bottles of hydrogen peroxide solution at 3%, one cup of baking soda, and a goodly amount of dishwashing soap."

Three hours, two shampoos, three thorough rinses, and a good drying with old towels later and he didn't smell as bad. The smell wasn't all gone, but it was a sight better than it was before. He would not be sleeping in the bedroom until it was gone. We cleaned up the bath area and walked on home. Halfway there, Harold found a patch of dust and proceeded to flop himself all in it. Maybe that would help some. We'd see. In any case, he slept on the porch that night. It took two days before he was tolerable to be around. But river swimming and running with the horses in the sun and rolling in warm meadow grass did the trick.

Finally Thursday arrived. The party was set to start at eight, so we had time to prepare. And by we I mean me since CC was at work all day. I mixed ground beef with seasonings and garlic and made patties, putting them on a tray with plastic wrap between the layers. Big, thick, slices of Sweet Vidalia onions got cut and covered. All that went in the fridge with the hot dogs.

Mom and Dad showed up and helped out. Mom got the serving/eating stuff ready, you know, the paper plates, napkins, heavy-duty plastic forks and knives, plastic cups, condiments and pickle slices, and two big trashcans with fresh liners. Mom also chopped some sweet onion to go on hot dogs.

Dad and I worked on getting the charcoal ready to light. He also brought a pot of his famous hot dog chili and big bowl of finely chopped coleslaw, all fresh made, for those so inclined.

By fifteen minutes after seven, big plastic tubs and ice were delivered by three A.S.S. members. They emptied ice over cans of beer and soft drinks.

CC was later than usual leaving work but finally got to the house at half past. Mom got out a big, deep lasagna pan to put cooked burgers in, and another baking dish for the cooked hot dogs. Then she set the oven temp at 250° and thus the party was officially begun.

I had decided against having the party at The Shed. I wanted to keep everyone close and easy to get to in case the killer tried to pull anything.

Cars were beginning to pull in. Detectives Love and Hepcutts arrived and did a fine job of not looking like the po-po. I hollered out people's names when they arrived and made introductions for those who didn't know each other. Conversation noise got louder, so that's always a good thing, right?

Our first possible arrived. It was Faith Johnson. I made sure to personally take her around and introduce her to the detectives. Behind Faith's back, I gave them the high-sign upon which giving Charlene and Mick got super chatty and found out all about the girl.

Burgers and dogs started coming off the grill, and Mom, having buttered and warmed all the burger buns, helped CC put a dog in each steamed bun. Dad managed to slip a dog to Harold who, of all things, was minding his manners and getting all the petting and belly rubbing he could stand from the growing crowd.

"Adman, how do you keep your dog's fur so silky?" hollered one guest.

I began. "First, you manage to get the dog sprayed by a skunk…" Everybody started laughing. "Then you get a big tub of warm water…" And that's as far as I got because they knew what the rest of the story would be.

I had already set up a keyboard in the living room and others brought instruments, so a mini jam was going on already.

Around nine our second possible killer showed up. "Ro-Ro!" I hollered. "How are you doing?"

She was just fine and said as much at which point I grabbed her elbow and began making introductions again. Another high sign to Love and Hepcutts and another awesome chat followed.

Misha texted me he was on his way. It had been our plan to have him arrive late. When he texted he was coming, I was to start setting the stage for why he was late. So I did.

"Hey, everybody!" I hollered until the din died down. "Misha is on his way. He's bringing a bottle of wine."

One of the members of the Amateur Sleuth Society saw his cue. "You mean the one he got sent by that fan-girl?"

"That's the one!"

During that exchange, Love watched Ro-Ro and Hepcutts watched Faith for any reactions on their parts to that announcement.

Then Ty could be heard to say, "I didn't think Misha was going to be able to make it. He's not been feeling good for a day or so."

That's when Ro-Ro's head whipped around and she said, "Misha? Sick? Should he be coming if he is contagious?"

Ty answered. "He don't got no fever or nothing like that. I told him it was prolly just a twenty-four-hour bug. He was a bit nauseous and pale, shaking a little. Saw him this afternoon. Seemed to be okay."

"I just hope he isn't dying of something exotic and gonna kill the rest of us," Ro-Ro said.

Love and Hepcutts took note of that little exchange. Then I said, "He'll be here in about thirty minutes and we can all see for ourselves."

And sure enough, thirty minutes later I get a text from Misha:

```
Outside. Coming in. Bottle half empty.
```

That's when I gave the high sign again to the detectives and the A.S.S.'s. David, who'd been making nice with Faith, took her by the elbow to go "get more beer". Chip and Gerry had been chatting up Ro-Ro and managed to maneuver her closer to the drinks. Love and Hepcutts, seeing the high sign themselves, walked over to get more to drink. And in walked Misha with his beeg entry.

Waving his half bottle of wine above his head, he announced, "'Allo! 'Allo! I haf arrive. Zee party may now beegeen."

Carl hollered, "Hey, is that the famous wine I've been reading about all over social media?"

"Eees the veddy same."

"Where's the cookies?" yelled Arturo.

"I ate two yesterday and Cloootch ate two. Coom to tink of it I seenk we got sick from sugar high and zat make us sick. Faith! Ro-Ro! Adman! Hey, everybody. Adman, who are zeez loooovleee ladies here?" He held out his hand for the shaking by Love and Hepcutts, who smiled big, and acted all impressed and such as that.

"Who is Cloootch, Misha?" Ro-Ro asked.

"He is my dog."

Ro-Ro looked horrified. "Is he okay now?"

"Like me," Misha nodded.

Then Love thought she'd stir the pot a bit. "What's this wine? Is it special?"

Misha said, in a stage whisper, "Zees guuurrrll I know, she is beeg fan…beeeeeEEG fan. She send me special bottle nyze wine a few weeks ago."

"I would've thought you would have already drank the whole thing by now," Ro-Ro said somewhat angrily. "Why did you wait to drink it?"

"Weeeell, I tayle you true. I been beezee-beezee-beezee. Forget. Zeen I remember cookies and zee the bottle and, as they say, *eto vse chto ona napisala*… errrr…zat's all she wrote."

"Oh." Seems she didn't like the reason, but what could she do about it? Nothing, that's what.

"Charlene, dear. You want?" Misha held out the bottle and waggled it at her. "Mick? You like, too? Yes? Say yes."

"I would love a sip of that famous wine." Mick said the same and both she and Charlene Love held out their empty glasses for some.

Faith was not watching any of this. She was busy deciding if she was going to have another hot dog. Mind made up, she was pouring on the mustard and heaping on the slaw. She turned to take a bite just as Misha was pouring the detectives a sip. He held out the bottle to Faith and she nodded yes. He poured her some and by now there was only a small sip left in the bottle.

Misha held it up to the light and, swaying a bit, examined the bottom of the bottle, saying, "Ro-Ro? Lassss zip. You want it?"

Ro-Ro shook her head no, but we all watched her watch Charlene and Mick and Faith, and even Misha. He held out the bottle to me, "Jaaaahn. You wan last zip?"

"Heck yeah." I grabbed the bottle and turned it up. But it wasn't to be. Ro-Ro pretended to stumble into me, knocking the bottle out of my hand and onto the floor. Tumbling end over end, wine flung out. Harold was not slow. He was licking it up and Ro-Ro was trying to drag him away from the wine.

"No, Harold!" she hollered. "Wine is not for dogs. No! Stop, Harold, stop!" But it was too late and Ro-Ro just stared at Harold like she'd just lost her very own best friend.

Slowly turning from Harold, Ro-Ro picked up the bottle, faced Misha, and screamed. "It's all your fault." She swung the bottle at Misha. He ducked and she swung again. He jumped back and grabbed the bottle from her. She lunged at Misha, clawing at his face, still screaming. "You stole from me. You need to die. Now you've killed Clutch and Harold."

Misha was laughing, not because it was funny, but because he couldn't believe what she was doing. Love and Hepcutts jumped in and, with the help of

Carl, Arturo, Leland, and Gerry, got her subdued on her stomach and in handcuffs.

Did that shut her up? No, it did not. Ro-Ro just kept on blaming Misha about poor Harold's upcoming death. I knelt beside Ro-Ro on the floor.

"Roxanne, what are you talking about? Harold just drank some wine. And only a little bit at that. Wine won't kill a dog. Are you okay?"

Roxanne cried and cried, mumbling, "Harold! Clutch! Poor Harold. Oh, Clutch, Clutch. Harold."

Hearing his name, Harold wiggled through the crowd of legs to find her, then licked her face.

"See? He's okay," I said. "Ro-Ro, why do you think he'll die?"

"Because the wine was poisoned, that's why. Misha was supposed to drink it. Not Harold. N-n-n-not Harold."

Spontaneous admission of guilt in front of at thirty-five witnesses who could hear it. I think Love and Hepcutts' case just got all sewed up. Misha was still confused…or at least acted like he was, but he's Russian and knows sneaky tactics of interrogation… or else was simply milking his beeg entry for all it was worth.

"Why you want me dead? What I do to you?"

Roxanne stared at him like he was insane. "You know what you did. Don't pretend you don't."

By this time, the mini jam in the living room was done and everybody was jockeying for a position to look at the killer on the floor like it was a movie. We had burgers and dogs, we just needed buttered popcorn now.

Roxanne looked at every face in the circle above her. "You just wait. He'll cheat you, too. They all do that. Just steal and steal and steal from you. And do they ever say they're sorry? No."

André said, "What did Misha steal from you?"

"He stole my hook. I've heard him use it in several songs since we played together that time at Joe's Jazz Jam." She whipped angry eyes at Misha who was now truly confused. "You remember. Say you remember. I know you remember."

"What hook?"

She laughed. "You want me to sing the notes here? Now? In front of everybody? 'Cause I will."

"Yes, please."

And so she did. But only a few in the room understood what she had done and we were horrified. So, I thought I'd help Love and Hepcutts a little further. I knelt down again beside Ro-Ro.

"Roxanne. Did Barry and Mario and Angela also steal your hooks?"

"Yes. Barry wouldn't sign a contract to play on my original song when I had it recorded. Then I heard him play part of it at a gig.

"And Mario. Do not get me started on Mario. He recorded me in his studio and then sold the music to somebody to use in their song. I only happened to hear it on the radio one day. So I got no royalties from that."

"And Angela? What did she do?"

"I went to her songwriting club and she made a recording of it and put it on the club's Facebook page. She did not get my permission to use it and that was copyright infringement, plain and simple."

I stood and stared down at her. "Roxanne, I hate to break it to you, but in Misha's case, the hook you thought you came up with is part of a song that was written back in the early 1900s. It was called 'Bill Bailey'. You probably learned it as a music exercise in school. Copyright ended on that a long time ago."

David, angry as a wet cat, said, "That means Misha didn't break the law or steal from you. And I bet Barry didn't either."

"Or Mario. He doesn't place anything with the record labels. He only deals with independent artists and he'd never sell you out," Leland shouted. "And royalties? Really? From radio play? That shows how much you know about the music business."

Then Leland stood up straight and like a minor god on Olympus, pointed a condemning finger at Roxanne and thundered, "Which P.R.O. are you signed up with? Huh? Or are you signed to a publisher or a label? Huh?"

Roxanne looked confused and when she did, everybody burst out laughing at her. Then somebody from the crowd hollered out, "All this for some nonexistent royalties. Are you stupid?"

I shook my fist at her. "Angela Peterson was only trying to give you more exposure and giving you a nice and warm Atlanta welcome. You knew she was recording her club meetings and always gets permission before posting." I turned to Love and Hepcutts. "If you look at Angela's email and messages and texts, I bet you find that permission."

Then Gerry asked the really big question. "Have you sent anybody else any poison potables and comestibles?"

The room went quiet as we waited for an answer. Roxanne, squirming against the cuffs, only asked, "What are those?"

"Drink and food. Have you sent any more?"

She cut sly eyes at Gerry. "No, I haven't."

"Are you sure, you little witch?" Gerry was making no bones about his opinion of her.

Leland quoted Latin at her. "*Falsus in uno, falsus in omnibus.*"

"Yes, I'm sure," she hollered at him, then gave another sly grin, but this time to Love who knew what Roxanne was thinking.

Love said loud enough for all to hear, "I bet you think this confession of yours won't hold up in a court of law because you weren't read your rights. Let me tell you, you little twit, you made a completely spontaneous confession. It wasn't me or my partner questioning you. Only your friends."

Roxanne's eyes got real big and she simply said two things. First: Huh. Second: I want an attorney. She clamped her mouth shut, but it was too late, she'd done confessed to everybody.

Love and Hepcutts lifted Roxanne from the floor and plunked her in a chair. They then announced they would have everybody write, sign, and date statements as to what they saw and heard here this evening while they waited on transport to take Roxanne to where she could be interrogated.

CC and Mom rounded up paper and pens and next thing you know we had people sitting around the table, scratching out their versions.

Love said, "Listen up. Nobody talk to each other about this. Only write what you know, you saw, you heard. Nothing else." Hepcutts kept a watchful eye on that process.

It was then I remembered what happened at Mario's funeral. Roxanne had overheard some of The Amateur Sleuth Society discussing the murders in the past. Like a thunderbolt, two things came back to my mind.

> Roxanne said, "Why did **she** kill those people?"
>
> I answered, "It wasn't a she. It was a he. And he did it because they each dissed him."
>
> "So he committed murder because he got his panties in a twist? His ego was hurt? Nobody is gonna kill for that. They might kill cuz somebody **stole something**. But getting dissed?"

All this time and the clue is finally registering in my brain. What an idiot.

Dad brought me a burger and said, "You'll need this." The slab of onion was so big I didn't even have to lift the bun to see it. He was right. I needed this as I'd forgotten to eat all evening.

Mom got to talking to Detectives Love and Hepcutts. They hit it off just fine by talking shop, you know, about substances that will kill.

Transport came and went, the detectives following in their car with a whole sheaf of statements. A jam had started up back in the living room, but this time it was in memory of our good friends Barry, Mario, and Angela. Harold lay at the feet of the piano player, only occasionally barking his pleasure at a certain turn of phrase.

Mom and Dad offered to help clean up, but CC and I sent them on home. They had a long drive and were already tired.

Everybody else but Misha was gone by half-past one. He was still reliving his beeg entry. We three sat around the kitchen table laughing, sadly, but so very happy the killing spree was over.

"Misha," CC said, "how did you manage to make yourself look so pale when you arrived?"

"Babeee powhdur."

"It worked great. Good job. Now I'm going to bed because some people around here got to get up early to work."

She gave us both kisses, Misha on the cheek, me on the lips, and headed off to bed with Harold following her.

"Harold!"

Harold knew what I wanted and why, turned around, and headed back my way.

"Back porch, Harold."

Misha gave me the stink eye. I said, "Look, Harold had a disagreement with a skunk and he is not yet bedroom ready."

But I was. Misha crashed on the sofa and I headed back to the bed. A few minutes later I heard the back porch door open and toenails clack-clack across the floor to the living room. So, Harold gets to snuggle with Misha tonight. Misha's poor nose.

I didn't care. I fell asleep just as CC rolled over and wrapped her arms around me.

Outro Notes

The names of the victims in *Death on the Downbeat* are based on real people who gave me permission to use their names in this book, but the stories about the characters have nothing to do with the people themselves. For instance, Barry Lamon in real life is a guitar player. He will be surprised to find himself to be a flugelhorn player, and so on.

MALE VICTIM ONE **Barry Lamon**

MALE VICTIM TWO **Mario Alberto Mireles**

FEMALE VICTIM THREE **Angela Peterson**

MALE VICTIM FOUR **Misha Stefanuk**

DETECTIVE **Charlene Love**

RED LIGHT CAFÉ: The real-life owners of the famous club in Midtown Atlanta are **Michael and Ellen Chamberlain**. The Gordon Vernick Jazz Jam, held there each Wednesday night, was the inspiration for the Wednesday Jazz Jam in this book. Michael and Ellen are huge supporters of live music and the author knows them very well. When the author told them she wanted to put them in the book, they were all for it and think it is a hoot.

DOG: "Harold" is played by Misha Stefanuk's real dog, Coco, a sweetie pie if ever there was one.

DON'T LET THIS SMILE FOOL YA
VERSE1:
C/Gm/Ab7 8-bar Blues

It's hard to think when I got a
man on my mind
Don't let this smile
fool ya
I'm tight as a drum with
Memories of love, aaah
ahh. Don't let this smile
fool ya
They say what you see is
what you get, but
Don't let this smile
fool ya

VERSE2:
He called me baby, sugar pie,
honey pot.
Don't let this smile
fool ya
He said "Come on, Hot Mama,
show me whatcha got."
Don't let this smile
fool ya
Blue eyes, "I love you",
starry dreams gone with the morning
Dew

BRIDGE:

You see this smile
Bright as the sun
Listen to me Good
My heart's on the run
Yeah So, don't, don't, don't, don't
no, no, no, no
Don't let this smile
fool ya

VERSE3:

Have I seen better days?
Too late for goodbye
Don't let this smile fool ya
Faceless nights, Nameless fears
Don't let this smile fool ya.
Love burns bright, then
comes the tears, so
Don't let this smile

OUTRO:

The night was hot
The night was hot
Don't let this smile
fool ya
His eyes too blue
His eyes too blue
His eyes too blue, Mama
Don't let this smile
Fool ya

Lyrics: Angela K. Durden
Publisher: Second Bight Publishing
© 2012

INTRO:
| AbM7 Bb7
  Db7/B Cm7 |
| Eb7/Db Dm7b5
  Fm/Ab G7 |

|Cm   EbM7 |Fm/Ab   Gsus7 |
V1: I cry over puppies.   I cry over kittens.
|Abm7 G/Cm |Fm/G   Cm/G G |
  I even cry over   spilt milk.
|Cm   EbM7/Bb |Db/Ab   G7+ |
  But no matter   how hard I try, I

6/4 |DbM7   Dm7b5   Cm7 **4/4**
  can't seem to cry over   you.

TURNAROUND: | AbM7 Bb7 Db7/B Cm7 |
** | Eb7/Db Dm7b5 Fm/Ab G7 |**

  |Cm   EbM7 |Fm/Ab Gsus7
V2: I cry when my groceries are bagged upside down.
|Abm7 G/Cm |Fm/G |Cm/G |G
I even cry over burnt toast.
|Cm   EbM7/Bb |Db/Ab   G7+
But no matter   how hard I try,
|DbM7   Dm7b5 |Cm7   Bb7 |
I can't seem to cry   over you.

I CAN'T SEEM TO CRY | Key Cm | Tempo: Slow Ballad   **PAGE 2 OF 2**

© 2018 Lyrics and Melody Angela K, Durden | Composition Alan Dynin | Second Bight Publishing

INTRO TO BRIDGE: ‖: |EbM7 Ab/Eb | EbM7 Gb/Eb |:‖

BRIDGE:

|EbM7   Ab/Eb | EbM7   Gb/Eb |
Cross my heart and hope to die. *(rit.)*

EbM7 Ab/Eb | EbM7 Gb/Eb | Abm7 | F#m6/ | CM7|
Stick a needle in my eye   if   I   lie.

|Dm7 G7 | Eb   /D Cm | *(rit.)*
Yes, no matter how hard I   try,

|Gb   E   D |Db#4
I can't seem to cry over   you.

TURNAROUND: |AbM7 Bb7 Db7/B Cm7 |
             | Eb7/Db Dm7b5 Fm/Ab G7 |

SOLOS TO BRIDGE INTRO; BRIDGE TO OUTRO:

(rit.) |Cm   EbM7 |Fm/Ab   Gsus7 |
V1:   I cry over puppies. I cry over kittens.

|Abm7   G/Cm
      I even cry   over...   over... over...

Lyrics: Angela K. Durden
Publisher: Second Bight Publishing
© 2018

BOOKS BY Durden Kell
Whitfield, Nebraska
A Benjamin Turner Novel
(2015)

Death in E minor 9[mm]
(2020)

BOOKS BY Angela K. Durden

Eloise Forgets How to Laugh
(2004)

A Mike and His Grandpa Story: Series
Heroes Need Practice, Too!
(2006, hardback; 2012, paperback)

A Mike and His Grandpa Story:
The Balloon That Would Not Pop!
(2012)

Opportunity Meets Motivation:
Lessons From Four Women Who Built
Passion Into Their Lives and Careers
(2010, out of print)

Men! K.I.S.S. Your Resume
and Say Hello to a Better Job
(2013, audio book)

Men! K.I.S.S. Your Resume
and Say Hello to a Better Job
(2013)

9 Stupid Things People Do
to Mess Up Their Resumes
(2000, out of print)

First Time For Everything
(2018)

Do Not Mistake This Smile
(2018)

Music Business Survival Manual (2018)

Navigating the New Music Business
as a DIY and Indie
(2015)

Conversations in Hyperreality —
and Other Thoughts Umberto Eco and
Dave Barry Never Had
(2019)

Dancing at the Waffle House
(2018)

Nagging Women and Clueless Men
(2017)

Music by Angela K. Durden
Caviar for One | Album (2019)
Spotify | Amazon Music
Other streaming portals
CD with liner notes booklet from author

From Blue Room Books
blueroombooks.com
blueroombooks@outlook.com

Jedwin Smith
I AM ISRAEL Lions and Lambs of the Land
(2018)

A Marine and a Journalist Walk Into a Bar
(2021)

Alan Ray White
Rock Around The Block (2019)

1960's Pop icon Len Barry
Prose and Cons
(2021)

W.F. Whitson
The Librarian: Intrigue at RAF Greenham
(2021)

Mike Shaw
The Musician (2021)

ISBN: 978-1-950729-13-5

DEATH on the DOWNBEAT
BLUEROOMBOOKS.COM
DECATUR, GEORGIA
978-1-950729-13-5

Made in the USA
Columbia, SC
01 August 2021

42775792R00107